F
Heath, Monica.
The legend of Blackhurst

The Legend of
Blackhurst

The Legend of **Blackhurst**

Monica Heath

THORNDIKE
CHIVERS

This Large Print edition is published by Thorndike Press®, Waterville, Maine USA and by BBC Audiobooks, Ltd, Bath, England.

Published in 2005 in the U.S. by arrangement with Maureen Moran Agency.

Published in 2005 in the U.K. by arrangement with the author.

U.S. Hardcover 0-7862-7235-X (Romance)
U.K. Hardcover 1-4056-3250-X (Chivers Large Print)
U.K. Softcover 1-4056-3251-8 (Camden Large Print)

The text of this Large Print edition is unabridged.
Other aspects of the book may vary from the original edition.

Set in 16 pt. Plantin by Minnie B. Raven.

Printed in the United States on permanent paper.

British Library Cataloguing-in-Publication Data available

Library of Congress Cataloging-in-Publication Data

Heath, Monica.
     The legend of Blackhurst / Monica Heath.
        p. cm.
     ISBN 0-7862-7235-X (lg. print : hc : alk. paper)
     1. Mansions — Fiction.   2. Louisiana — Fiction.
   3. Plantation life — Fiction.   4. Missing persons —
   Fiction.   5. Mothers and daughters — Fiction.
   6. Large type books.   I. Title.
   PS3558.E264L44 2005
   813′.54—dc22   2004061504

The Legend of
Blackhurst

Chapter ONE

Standing quietly in the room that once belonged to my mother, as I gaze out upon the billowing cane fields which thrive in the midst of Louisiana's black-fingered bayou country, I can believe, at last, that this is where I belong.

Even the legend, kept secret from me for so long, holds no terror for me now. I can see in my mind's eye the delicate webs woven by giant spiders imported from China more than a hundred years ago and released in the huge live oaks that still shelter Blackhurst's gardens, where they created a glittering canopy beneath which that first bride was to be married.

The story has it that on the day of her wedding, the plantation slaves were provided with bellows and pails of gold and silver dust with which they turned the webs into a shimmering fantasy. Not to be outdone by his wealthy Creole neighbors whose extravagances he had mimicked, my ancestor, who was the bridegroom, had ordered a thousand lanterns hung to light the gilded gardens. Dancing cloths were laid over the lawns and a New Orleans caterer famous for his bouillon, daube glacé and incomparable nougat, had brought his staff to Blackhurst well in advance of the ceremony to prepare a bounteous feast for the more than five hundred invited guests.

But in spite of these elaborate preparations, undertaken at great expense by that long-ago Blackhurst, the marriage was never consummated.

That same afternoon, shortly before the nuptial pair were to say their vows, a tragedy occurred — a tragedy which was to haunt Blackhurst Hall for more than a century. It was Gabe who finally told me the horrifying details of that tragically romantic tale; Gabe Guirlande, whose presence at the old house was first revealed to me in a letter from my mother.

She mentioned him again in the last letter I was ever to receive from her and, perhaps for that very reason, his name clung to my memory. I had not the least inkling then that the two of us were destined to meet and that, as a result of that meeting, I would find myself enmeshed in the chain of events generated by the old legend.

I awakened to the dreary moan of fog horns the day I received that last puzzling letter from my mother. Outside my window, where, as a child, I could see the Union Street cable car turn around at Vallejo and Larkin, a bedraggled, black pigeon perched, its head cocked archly to one side. One instant the bird was there, regarding me through the misted panes with a fiery eye; the next instant it was gone, fading into the dense tulle fog as though it had never been there at all.

Thinking back to that dismal, gray morning, I now imagine the bird to have been an omen; a tattered, black harbinger of evil sent by some mysterious fate to warn me.

At the time, however, my main concern was for my mother. It had been nearly three weeks since I had last heard from her and my first waking thought was a prayer that today the letter would finally arrive — the letter she had promised to write when she called me from St. Bridges, while waiting for one of my cousins to meet the bus she had taken there from the New Orleans airport.

The two of us had known when my aunt, Seena Verret, had summoned my mother to help care for their ailing father that there was small hope for his recovery. Nevertheless, and in spite of the gravity of my grandfather's condition, it was not like my mother to break a promise she had made.

To add to my growing anxiety, I had tried on several occasions to contact her by telephone, only to be told by the lazily drawling voice of the St. Bridges operator that the line to Blackhurst Hall had recently blown down in a windstorm. The line, a "ring down" out of St. Bridges, was maintained by the plantation, the operator had said, her ingratiating tone seeming to suggest that broken lines were to be expected, under the circumstances.

It had all sounded rather primitive — and not a little bit frightening, when I realized there was no other way I could reach my mother, apart from my letters which had so far gone unanswered.

I could not help asking myself why. Why had my mother neglected her promise to write to me? What had happened to cause her to break that promise? Had she become so deeply involved, helping Seena care for my grandfather who had been devastated by a massive stroke, that she had no time left for me?

Becoming aware that my thoughts bordered dangerously on self-pity, I scolded myself aloud, thinking that it would never do for me to show up with a long face at the modeling agency which handled my bookings. "All right, Miss Tracey O'Toole, that will do."

At nineteen, I was just beginning to make a name of sorts for myself as a fashion model, thanks to Guy Lannin, the photographer who had "discovered" me. A small, rotund man old enough to be my father, Guy had purchased the house next door to ours shortly after my father had died.

Although I am not what you might call beautiful or even pretty, Guy saw something in me he wanted to express through his camera, assuring me when I hesitated to pose for him that first time, that my high, prominent cheekbones, cloud of black hair and light green eyes were highly photogenic. Perhaps more importantly, though, I was tall for a girl, with the boyishly slender body and long, coltish legs that were currently in vogue.

"You'll be a smashing success, Tracey, wait and see," he had told me.

It had all happened so quickly that I was not certain even yet I liked the role I found

11

myself playing before the cameras and on the runways. But my mother and I needed the extra money I was able to earn as a model and so it had seemed expedient for me to put aside my plan to enroll in a good business school, at least for the time being.

Now, taking a last look out through the window to make certain the strange, hungry-looking bird had not returned, I slid reluctantly from my warm bed. The house, which was located on what Mrs. Costain, the elderly recluse who lived across the street from us, liked to refer to as "the poor man's side of Russian Hill," echoed emptily around me as I made my way down the back stairs to the brightly papered kitchen, which seemed suddenly cheerless without my mother's smiling presence there to greet me.

Putting on a kettle of hot water for my morning coffee, I went to the front door, as was my usual custom, to bring in the morning paper. Glancing toward the street, I was surprised to see Mrs. Costain scuttling toward me out of the thick mist, a faded wrapper clutched tightly across her scrawny breast. There was something furtive in her manner, which alarmed me.

"What is it, Mrs. Costain?" I called anxiously. "Can I help?"

Flinging a last furtive look across her shoulder, she came up the steep porch steps, her small, dark eyes flashing in her wrinkled face.

"I was afraid *he* might be watching," she gasped as she sidled past me into the house. "Come on in, honey, before he sees us. I've got something for you. Something he's been waiting and watching for. But it's all right, deary. I caught onto his little game and beat him to it."

"What on earth are you talking about?" I stifled a sudden urge to shy away from the strange old woman when I recalled the stories the neighbors told about her eccentric behavior.

"The man who's been spying on you almost ever since your mother went away, deary," Mrs. Costain said. "This is what he was after." Reaching a clawlike hand into the bosom of her wrapper, she withdrew a letter.

There was no mistaking the pale blue envelope, engraved with my mother's initials. Her handwriting, cherished and familiar, served to further identify it.

Here, then, was the letter whose arrival I had so eagerly anticipated.

I said accusingly, "You took this from my box?" reaching to take it from the old woman's unsteady fingers. "What right had you to do that?" I went on when I had glanced at the address to make certain it was meant for me.

"No need to get huffy, honey," Mrs. Costain pouted. "If I hadn't taken it in for you, he'd have got *his* wily hands on it."

It occurred to me then that the aggravating crone was attempting to cover up some minor misdeed of her own by suggesting that someone else had tried to rob my mailbox.

"Who is this man you keep referring to, Mrs. Costain?" I asked, making an effort to curb my growing impatience, wanting nothing more at the moment than to be rid of her so I could be alone to read the long-awaited letter.

"The man who's been watching your house, poking into your letter box when he thinks no one is looking."

"I've seen no one," I stated matter-of-factly.

"How could you when you're gone from morning to night? I'd have brought your letter over sooner. But I was already in bed when I heard you come in last night. I saw no sense in inconveniencing myself when it could just as well wait until morning," she added defiantly, flashing me an aggrieved look above lips that had become tightly pursed.

"You've seen this man looking into my letter box?" I asked, ignoring her self-pitying look, even as I wondered how much of her dubious story I dared to believe.

"Would I have taken it upon myself to watch for the postman so I could take in your mail before he got to it, if I hadn't made certain first that was what he was after?"

"I don't know, Mrs. Costain," I said truthfully. "I really don't know."

"Well, take it from me, honey, what I'm telling you is the absolute truth," she retorted in those same aggrieved tones. "He looked like a foreigner of some kind to me, with his tanned skin and black eyes. His hair was black, too; as black as the Devil's own. He's up to no good where you're concerned, mark my words." Her voice had altered, becoming slightly threatening, as though, I thought, she had decided it would serve me right if I should come to some harm as a result of my skepticism.

I did not know whether to scold the old woman or to thank her graciously, as I nudged her gently toward the door.

"I know you meant well," I said uncertainly.

"Maybe you'd ought to see what your mother has to say," she said slyly. "Maybe she mentions him in her letter."

"I'll let you know," I said, giving her a gentle push through the open doorway.

I had started to close the door after her when she turned to poke her grizzled head through the narrow opening. "I'll watch for the postman again today, dearie, just in case he's still hanging around the neighborhood."

"That won't be necessary," I said firmly, closing the door before she could protest, thinking as I did so that the neighbors had been right about her; she was definitely a bit odd in a way which could very well prove to be a nuisance if I permitted her to persist in her strange notions.

Determined not to take too seriously her remarks about the man she claimed to have seen rummaging through my letter box, I tore open the seal on my letter, the irritation I had felt with the unpredictable old woman swiftly dissipating as my gaze fell on my mother's familiar script.

My dear Tracey, the letter began. *It was my intention to write to you sooner. But I have had no opportunity to get a letter off to you until now. If it should happen that I must break this off before I have finished setting down what I must say to you, please bear with me. This ancient old house I once loved so dearly has become a house of death which has had its effect on us all.*

I regret to say that there is no hope whatsoever for your grandfather's recovery, the second paragraph stated with a fatalistic clarity so out of keeping with my mother's usual optimism that I found myself wondering briefly if she had written the letter, after all. *I have been told that death holds no dread for the very old; that it is only those of us who are still comparatively youthful who find it so terrible to live without hope. Perhaps I should tell you now that your grandfather's affairs have been placed in the hands of a local attorney who spends a great deal of time secluded with him in his sickroom. His name is Gabriel Guirlande, although those who live here prefer to call him Gabe Garland. As you may already have guessed from his name, he is a Cajun.*

No doubt this will dismay you, the letter continued. *But it has been decided that I shall remain here at Blackhurst Hall indefinitely.*

I broke off appalled. *It has been decided . . .* The words leapt up at me from off the page. Who at Blackhurst Hall had taken it upon themselves to influence my

17

mother to remain there? Was it my grand-father's attorney, Gabe Guirlande, who wanted her to stay? Or had her sister Seena taken it upon herself to dictate what she should do? In which case, why should my mother feel compelled, as the letter seemed to suggest, to listen to her?

Even as a child I had known there was friction between my mother and her older sister. It did not make sense to me even now that she would want to remain at Blackhurst Hall any longer than necessary.

Swiftly scanning the closely spaced lines, I searched for some clue to explain that strange decision which made her seem suddenly remote from me.

The library here is still much as I remember it, the letter continued. *The books that fascinated me as a child are still in their places. I doubt that anyone has bothered to look at them since then. I was always the bookworm in the family. Only last night, I delved into a volume of famous quotations I enjoyed as a young girl. The book fell open to the lines I made you memorize from Fuller's "Life of Monica."*

The letter ended there with an abruptness that left me stunned. There was no signature, nothing to signify that it had indeed been my mother who wrote the lines I had just read.

More puzzling still was her reference to the lines from Fuller which she seemed to imagine I should know. Try as I might, I could not recall ever having heard of them before.

What hold had Blackhurst Hall gained on her to cause her to dwell so persistently on thoughts of death and dying?

"It's a tyrannical old monstrosity," my mother had once said of the house. And, although there had been a certain fondness in her voice, I had not missed the shadow that passed behind her eyes, as though her memories of the life she had lived there, prior to her marriage to my father, were not altogether pleasant ones. "The attic is chock-full of mementos. Old songbooks filled with sentimental ballads and ancient prayer books spilling out dusty clusters of forget-me-nots and gardenias; bridal nose-gays, I should imagine, tucked away for safekeeping, their owners long since forgotten. There are even a few frayed remnants of the first bride's trousseau. She was to have been married in the acres and acres of gardens where the camellias still bloom after all of these years."

But it was not the flowers that had interested me; it was the bride who had caught my fancy, even then.

"What was her name?" I had wanted to know with all of the demanding perseverance of a nine-year-old. "Where is she now?"

"Her name was Amber, not that it really matters now," my mother said, that same dark shadow passing behind her eyes. "It all happened so long ago. She's been sleeping for years and years inside the old family vault."

"Will my cousins sleep there with her when they die?" I persisted, in a voice tinged with envy. "Will *I*?" I tacked on hopefully.

"The original tomb was sealed off ages ago," my mother said evasively. "But let's not dwell on death, shall we, darling. You're much too young to want to worry about such things."

"It had something to do with my wild cousins, I suppose," I said, disappointment turning my voice tart.

"A quartet of savages," my father, who rarely joined our conversations about the house and its occupants, said from his place beside the kitchen table. I think my mother had forgotten he was there, for she gave a little start. "It's easy to imagine them following in their father's footsteps," he went on ambiguously.

"Would that be so terrible?" my mother said in a voice that sounded slightly strained.

"I find it difficult even to imagine how a grown man could have been content to fritter his life away searching the swamps for Lafitte's lost treasure," my father had said then. "I'm not surprised his idle ways finally caught up with him. It's a shame some of the oil that's making the South rich today couldn't have sprung up on Blackhurst's worn-out acres, to help your father support Seena and her brood after Ves died. It can't have been easy for him, all of these years."

My mother had become grim-lipped, refusing to reply. Aware that they had forgotten about me, I looked on in confusion, too young to grasp the full implication behind my father's disapproval of a man who, had he lived, would have been my uncle, beyond the fact that Ves Verret had been a wastrel of sorts who had died in some mysteriously ignominious way as a result of what my father had once referred to as "a drunken Cajun brawl."

"They've strange ways of expressing themselves, the Cajuns," I remembered my father saying on yet another occasion. "They've a queer habit of selecting names

21

for their children that begin with the same letter or syllable, for instance, and that has led them woefully astray from the French heritage of which they profess to be so proud," he had explained when I had questioned him. "The Verret family has been addicted to the letter 'V' for years. *Valérien. Valsin. Valcour. Valmore. Valerie. Valmir*," he had recited when I had pressed him to tell me what some of their names were.

One branch of the family had strayed to follow the "R" line in the naming of their children, he had elucidated. *Regile. Ray. Rhea. Raymal. Ramide. Rita.* And there had been yet another branch which had followed the "M" line for *Marie, Mayard, Magda . . .*

And what of my cousins I wondered. What line had Seena followed in her naming of her half-Cajun offspring? Did their names all begin with "V," or had she chosen at random from among the vast array of exotic family names which apparently had been available to her?

All in all, I realized now how very little I knew of those who inhabited the ancient plantation house that had dominated their lives for more than a century, partly because of the rift between my mother and her older sister, which precluded any intimacy that might once have existed between them.

My mother had returned to Blackhurst Hall only once before in all of the years she had been away, when my Grandmother Blackhurst died. She had seemed different to me somehow when she returned to my father and me in San Francisco, following that first brief visit. There had been something secretive in her manner after that, whenever Blackhurst was mentioned, something as ambiguous as the mystery which confronted me now between the puzzling lines of her letter.

Chapter TWO

Remembering my early morning appointments, I folded the pages of the letter into the blue envelope and telephoned for a cab.

Back in my room, I slid into faded denim pants and matching jacket, flinging a scarf over the large rollers I still wore in my hair. Then, tucking my mother's letter into my tote bag, I quickly assembled the makeup items I would need to complete the day's shootings, tossing my brush and comb into the bag after them when the horn of the waiting cab sounded in the street below.

Mrs. Costain was watching from behind her ragged curtains when I went out the door. How much of the old woman's wild story of a black-haired stranger who was intent on robbing me of my mail could I believe, I wondered, her stubborn vigilance behind the curtained panes making me uneasy. Supposing such a man did exist, what possible reason could he have for wanting to steal my mother's letters from me, as Mrs. Costain seemed to imagine was the case?

Settling back against the cab's cushions, I took the monogrammed envelope from my tote bag and read the letter through again. With no signature to identify its author, it might have been sent by anyone who had access to my mother's monogrammed stationery and who was clever enough to imitate her handwriting. The familiar initials engraved at the top of the page prompted me to speak her name softly aloud.

"Lorainne Monica O'Toole." A queer excitement struck me as I realized that my mother's middle name was the same as the name in the title of the poem she had expected me to know.

Monica. Had she been attempting to convey some special message to me through the lines from Fuller? But it was preposterous even to imagine that she may have had something like that in mind, a small, logical corner of my mind argued. Why should she want to be so secretive when all she needed to do in order to convey her thoughts to me was to pick up a telephone and call me, or, in the event the line to Blackhurst Hall remained down indefinitely as seemed to be the case up to now, to take pen and paper in hand and set them down for me?

"Here you are, Miss." The cab driver's voice cut rudely across my teeming thoughts.

Nevertheless, I knew what I would do, and when Guy Lannin offered to drive me home late that evening from the fashionable restaurant where we had spent the better part of the day shooting a glossy fashion spread, I accepted gratefully, asking him if he would mind dropping me off at the branch library.

"I'll take a cab home from here," I told him when he offered to wait for me.

It was not until after he had driven away, the taillights of his station wagon disappearing into the long lines of traffic, that I remembered I had left my tote bag on the rear seat of his car. Not that it really mattered, I thought, turning to run quickly up the library steps. I did not need my mother's letter to know what I was after.

"*Bartlett's Familiar Quotations* should have what you want," the plump gray-haired woman behind the desk told me when I sought her assistance.

Leaving the desk in charge of a co-worker, she ushered me between the stacks to the rear of the room, where she reached to pull a worn red volume from a shelf above her head. Handing the book to me without comment, she returned to her station, leaving me alone to skim swiftly through its index.

A short while later, I was staring down at the single quotation the book contained from Fuller's *Life of Monica*, that same bewildering sense of uneasiness I had felt when I first read my mother's letter returning to haunt me.

Drawing near to her death, she sent most pious thoughts as harbingers to heaven, the dismaying passage read. *And her soul saw a glimpse of happiness through the chinks of her sickness-broken body . . .*

I read the lines through again. But it was no use. I knew with absolute certainty that I had never heard them before, in spite of my mother's apparent belief that she had made me memorize them as a child.

"I'm sorry. But it's already past our closing time." I glanced up to see the librarian hovering nervously at my elbow. "I hope you've had time to find what you were after."

"Yes. Yes, I did." Thanking her, I returned the book to its place on the shelf and went to the pay booth in the vestibule to call a taxi.

It was shortly after nine when I arrived home, noticing as I slid out of the cab that a faint, yellow light flickered behind the smudged panes of Mrs. Costain's second-floor bedroom. Candle light, I thought absently, marveling a little at the old woman's eccentricities, when I glimpsed her silhouette behind the tattered curtains.

Her continuing vigilance sent a queer little shiver of fear through me and, turning abruptly away from her invisible stare, I ran quickly up the steep porch steps, pausing to dip my fingers anxiously into my letter box. Disappointed to find that the box was empty, I stooped dejectedly to fumble for the extra key I kept hidden beneath the top step, the lights from an approaching car sweeping over me as it turned the corner to come toward me along the empty street.

Guy Lannin, I thought, when the car slowed to turn into the next-door drive. Evidently he had stopped somewhere after he had dropped me off at the library. Briefly I considered slipping through the tall hedge between our two houses to retrieve my tote bag. Then I decided against it, thinking that it could wait until morning, as the long hours spent before the cameras, sweltering beneath hot lights, caught up with me.

Unlocking the front door, I returned the

key to its hiding place and went into the house, making my way wearily into the kitchen, where I opened a can of soup and put it on the stove to heat while I went up to my room to change into my robe.

I was halfway up the narrow back stairs when somewhere above me a floorboard creaked. My first thought was that my mother had returned home unexpectedly and that even now, she was in her room, changing out of her trim, tweed travel suit into something more comfortable. Her room was at the rear of the house where her lights would not have been visible to me from the street below.

Running quickly upward, I called her name as I went. When there was no reply, I called a second time, my voice echoing out of the discomfiting silence above me.

There was a stealthy, shuffling sound somewhere in the shadows beyond the landing, and suddenly I was afraid as Mrs. Costain's dire warning flashed across my mind: *He's up to no good where you're concerned, mark my word.*

It was foolish to allow the peculiar old woman's strange imaginings to inhibit me, that small, logical corner of my mind told me. At the same time, I felt the hairs on my neck prickle in alarm, as some deep-seated intuitive sense sought to warn me.

Staying where I was, I listened. Out of the charged silence above me came the faint sound of a man's heavy breathing, I was certain of it.

Seized by an uncontrollable panic, I cried out sharply, "Who's there?"

He came at me, then, lunging out of the black shadows beyond the curve of the landing. Turning to run, my toe caught on the frayed runner as I flew downward and I went plunging, a hollow thud ringing in my ears as my head struck solidly against the plastered wall.

Vaguely, I felt myself being carried upward. The next thing I knew, I was lying on my bed, a nightmare pain pulsing behind my temple. Forcing open my eyes, I made out the dark form of a man looming over me, outlined in stark silhouette against the faint bluish glow of the nightlight which burned in the hall beyond the open doorway.

"Who are you?" I whispered numbly, thinking that I must be dreaming, that none of this could be real.

He started and, for a shattering instant, I imagined he was going to strike me. I jerked away from his raised hand, the violent motion triggering the blinding pain

30

that sliced behind my temple. I must have blacked out briefly for when I opened my eyes again, the man was kneeling beside me, and I felt his fingers fumbling at my throat.

Forcing back the thick, gray cloud which threatened to envelope me, I screamed.

At once, from somewhere below me, a man's voice answered my cry. "Tracey? In God's name what's happening?"

I felt the cruel fingers that had fastened themselves tightly about my neck withdraw abruptly. I held my breath as, for a tense moment, my assailant hesitated.

Then I let it out again on a relieved little cry, when he leaped to his feet and ran.

I tried to rise from my bed to follow him. But a wave of dizziness swept over me, and I fell back gratefully into the enveloping softness of that smothering, dark cloud.

When I opened my eyes again, Guy Lannin was beside me, my tote bag dangling loosely from his hand.

"Tracey, you're hurt!" Tossing the bag onto the bed beside me, he disappeared into the bathroom, returning a moment later with a wet towel which he pressed gently against my throbbing temple. "What happened, for God's sake?" He stared down anxiously at me. "Are you going to

31

be all right or shall I call a doctor?"

"Did you see him?" I gasped, when my senses had begun to clear.

"See who?"

"There was a man here when I came in. Mrs. Costain's black-haired stranger," I added vaguely. "He must have run out past you. That, or he went down the back way. Which means he had been here long enough to acquaint himself with the layout of the house."

For the first time, I noticed the room's disarray, wondering numbly what he had been after. My neat stacks of lingerie had been flung from their drawers; my small writing desk which stood beneath the window was a shambles. Even the closet had been ransacked, my dresses torn from their hangers and tossed carelessly onto the floor; my shoes pulled from their rack and thrown wildly about the room.

"It looks like the work of a madman," Guy said. "Did you get a look at him?"

I shook my head. Something cool and slithery crawled against my throat and I cried out, my fingers flying up to encounter a tangled strand of beads.

But I had not been wearing beads, I thought in stunned bewilderment, lifting my head to stare down at the tangled chain of honey-gold droplets in which tiny, hideous insects floated, trapped there in some past age to be preserved for posterity. I noticed then that the long strand had been carefully knotted to form a hangman's noose, the artfully tangled coils made all the more lethal by the lifelike perfection of the tiny flies and spiders encased in the softly polished globules.

Amber, that small, logical corner of my mind noted; noting, too, in that same calmly detached way, that the beads belonged neither to me nor my mother.

Where had they come from? Was the man who had attacked me a professional thief who carried his loot with him and who used the first implement that came into his hands in his effort to silence me?

"He tried to strangle you with your own beads," Guy said disbelievingly, stopping to examine the bruises on my throat.

I started to tell him the beads did not belong to me, but before I could speak, the doorbell jangled noisily across my bruised mind.

"Wait here." He was already hurrying toward the stairs.

Ignoring his command, I rose on shaky legs to follow him into the hall, leaning anxiously across the stairway's polished rail

33

to watch him disappear into the dark well below. A light flashed on, followed by a murmur of voices. A moment later, Mrs. Costain appeared, her small, black eyes glittering triumphantly up at me out of their deeply seamed crevices.

"I told you he was up to no good, dearie," the old woman gloated. "Aren't you glad now I paid you no mind when you asked me not to bother with your mail today? If I'd listened to you, he'd have got what he was after." Dipping scrawny fingers into the neck of her faded wrapper, she pulled out a letter.

I recognized the blue envelope instantly.

I shall never know what prompted me to remain silent about the beads when, a few moments later, the police arrived in response to Guy's call. Unless it was because it had occurred to me by then that they might have belonged to my mother after all; that they were, perhaps, a keepsake which she had kept hidden from me for her own private reasons.

In any case, the officer in charge seemed disinclined to believe Mrs. Costain's story about a tall dark stranger who had been intent on stealing my mother's letters from me.

"Listen, lady. If he was snooping around

Miss O'Toole's porch like you say, it wasn't her mailbox he was interested in. More likely he was making sure there was nobody at home here before he let himself inside."

It had been determined by then that the man had entered the house through either the front or the back door, using a master key, for there had been no windows broken, nothing at all to suggest he had entered violently.

Nor did anything appear to be missing.

"These guys win a few, lose a few," the officer commented, pausing to jot something in his notebook when I assured him that everything seemed to be intact, apart from my wildly scattered belongings.

Apparently, I had come onto the robber before he had had a chance to search the house, beyond my bedroom, which was the only room that had been disturbed.

"You were lucky this time, Miss," the officer said, when he and his companion had completed their investigation. "Chances are he won't be back."

Taking the officer at his word, since it could not have been anything but obvious to the robber that the house contained very little that was of value, I was relieved when everyone had finally gone, leaving me alone at last with my mother's letter.

The second note from her was brief, scarcely more than half a page written in a small, shaky script which filled me with a nervous apprehension even before I began to read.

My dearest daughter, the letter began. *I had no desire to burden you with my problems when I wrote to you earlier, for fear I would alarm you unnecessarily. But now it has become urgent that I see you. I have become ill and it now seems possible that I may die. It is my intention to contact your grandfather's attorney, Gabe Guirlande, at the first available opportunity, to let him know I have sent for you. Please come. I need you. Your loving mother.*

Partly because I was still stunned by the evening's jarring events, partly because my mother had never before, in her entire life, been seriously ill, it was a moment or two before the full impact of her letter hit me.

Then, suddenly, fear swept over me like an icy wind and my only thought was that I must go to her as swiftly as a plane could carry me.

Chapter THREE

It was late evening when I arrived before Blackhurst's rusted gates, only to find them locked securely against me. Behind me, the uncertain clatter of the retreating taxi faded swiftly into the eerie sounds arising from some nearby swamp; before me, beyond the oak-and-acorn-patterned panels, the pale drive wound like a stained ribbon through the deepening gloom cast by the giant pecan trees which lined it on either side.

No one at Blackhurst Hall knew of my arrival. When I had tried to reach the plantation by telephone to let my mother know I had received her message, the operator had told me there was still trouble with the lines. She had not known what the trouble was exactly, beyond the fact that no one at Blackhurst Hall had yet bothered to repair whatever damage had been done.

A growl of thunder came out of the west, obliterating the distant sounds of the fleeing taxi whose driver had seemed almost rude in his eagerness to escape, as though, I thought, he had sensed some dark threat hovering behind the unyielding gates.

"No one ever goes to Blackhurst Hall anymore," he had informed me when we left St. Bridges. "No one except Gabe Garland, that is."

Gabe Garland. The name kept cropping up, causing me to wonder what manner of man it belonged to. *A Cajun,* my mother had said of him in her letter. Perhaps because of the guarded remarks my father had made concerning Seena's husband, Ves Verret, and my half-Cajun cousins, I found myself visualizing him as savage, a hazily secretive figure stalking the marshes in search of lost treasure, in spite of the incongruities that particular picture seemed to pose when I paused to consider that Gabe Garland was my grandfather's attorney.

I said, when I caught the driver watching me in the taxi's rearview mirror, "I know no Gabe Garland."

"He was old man Blackhurst's attorney," the driver commented knowingly.

Was. My grandfather was dead, then. I was not greatly shaken, considering the fact that I had never met him, although I felt a certain sadness for my mother who, if she was ill as her letter had suggested, was in no condition to deal with a death in the family. Did that explain the morbid tone of her letters? Had she dreaded facing the imminent fact of my Grandfather Blackhurst's death?

The driver still watched me.

I said, "Perhaps I'll meet this Gabe Garland, then."

"Chances are." He glanced briefly at the road, his gaze coming back to my reflection in the mirror. "That is, if you stay."

"I'm Seena Verret's niece," I said then.

"Mayhap that will make a difference," he said obscurely, falling silent for the remainder of the twelve-mile journey which had cost me more than I could afford.

Now, standing alone before the plantation's barred gates, I could not stifle an involuntary little shudder as my gaze fell on a listing "No Trespassing" sign half-hidden behind the thick tangle of vines which clung to the crumbling brick wall at either side of the darkly rusted barriers. Fighting down a sudden wave of panic, I made out an ancient slave bell hanging above a post on which a large, tarnished mailbox was mounted, its weathered yoke all but hidden in the dense shadows of the huge old trees which overhung the mildewed masonry.

Reaching for the bell's frayed pull, I tugged tentatively at the loosely plaited fibers, noting with relief the fresh tire tracks marring the coarse gravel near the base of the post. Their presence seemed to suggest at least a modicum of normalcy. Then, upon releasing the rope, I peeked into the box to find that a packet of magazines and newspapers had been deposited inside.

Above my head, the bell's plaintive sound rose and fell softly, fading swiftly into the heavy silence that surrounded me. An instant later, a shrill cry, high and keening, like the voice of someone bereft, echoed out of the swamp. And, although I knew it to be the call of some strange bird, I could not help thinking of my dead grandfather, becoming painfully aware as I did so that I had come to a house of mourning.

When a few moments later it had become apparent to me that no one intended to respond to my summons, it seemed that I had no choice but to gather up my bags and pick my way as carefully as I could through the prickly vines which guarded a jagged break in the ancient wall, to the left of the sagging gates.

Sliding through the narrow opening, I pulled my bags through after me, the faint peal of the swaying slave bell dying on a soft tone that followed me like a warning whisper as I struck off bravely through the deeply shadowed pecan alley.

In the swamp, the keening bird had fallen silent. There was only the low-growling thunder and my own sudden, sharp awareness that from somewhere out of the stormy shadows, someone watched.

The gently curving drive took me in the direction of a dense palmetto thicket, visible beyond the black shadows cast by the overhanging pecans. Was it the black, beady stare of some crawling, swampland creature I felt following me? The question lurked in my mind, hurrying my footsteps.

Without warning, a dark shadow laced across my path; striped coils writhed to form a twisted pattern inches from my toes. *Snake,* said the calm, logical corner of my mind, but a wave of terror went through me when I recalled the tales I had heard of the poisonous reptiles that haunted the Louisiana bayou country. At the same time, and for no discernible reason, I was reminded of the amber beads which had been looped tightly around my neck when Guy Lannin had appeared to rescue me from the man who had lain in wait for me in the house in San Francisco.

I shivered and skirted the edge of the shell drive to keep my distance from the small, treacherous-looking serpent, watching it warily. There was a soft, rustling sound in the dense growth, and suddenly the snake veered toward me, slithering swiftly across the tightly packed shells, as though determined to find a mark for its tiny, flashing fangs.

I screamed then, in spite of myself, as a dreadful clap of thunder rent the air around me.

In that same instant, I saw the man, his bronzed face briefly illuminated by a streak of lightning.

Moving as swiftly as a cat, the man lunged past me to grind the snake's small, darting head beneath the stout heel of his boot. For an absurd moment, I had the sensation that none of it was real, that I was back again in my bed in San Francisco, caught up in the grip of some hideous nightmare.

Then he spoke in a matter-of-fact voice, and the spell was broken.

"Coral snake." He stared intently at me through that eerie light. "What in God's name are you doing out here in the marshes?"

Something undefined in his manner

made me cautious. I said, "I might ask you the same thing."

"I belong here." He looped limp coils across the toe of his boot, flinging the crushed reptile aside with a swiftly violent motion, as though to emphasize his laconic comment.

"I'm Tracey O'Toole," I said then, deciding that if he belonged on Blackhurst soil, he must be one of my cousins.

A subtle change came over him. "You're a long way from home, aren't you?" he said guardedly.

"I've come to be with my mother, Lorainne O'Toole," I added, when he continued to watch me in that same suspicious way. "How is she? Take me to her."

"I've no idea what you're talking about," he said with a maddening incomprehension.

"She wrote to tell me she's been taken ill and needs me," I told him. I became suddenly aware of features that seemed oddly satanic beneath hair that was as black as night.

He looked like a foreigner of some kind to me, with his tanned skin and black eyes, Mrs. Costain had said of the stranger she claimed to have seen lurking around my letter box. Her words returned to haunt me now, making me unconscionably aware of the man's saturnine good looks. He was tall, with a strange, dark splendor that had an oddly compelling effect on me, even as an urge to flee from him took hold of me, and it required all my courage to stay where I was, pinned beneath his challenging stare.

"There's no one at Blackhurst Hall, apart from Seena Verret and her family," he finally said.

It occurred to me on a little wave of relief that he was not one of my wild cousins after all, and I was able to tell myself then that I was merely being fanciful to have imagined, even briefly, that he might have been the man Mrs. Costain had seen poking into my letter box in San Francisco.

Whoever the man who confronted me now might prove to be, I would not be intimidated by his handsome looks, I thought, far more bravely than I felt.

I said, a note of defiance edging my voice, "Then perhaps it hasn't been your good fortune to meet my mother," part of my mind labeling him a Cajun, savage, no doubt, as were the cousins whom I had never met, if my father's opinion of them should prove to be valid.

I thought then to ask his name.

44

"I'm Gabriel." He smiled in a cynical way, as though he anticipated the peculiar sense of irony his dark looks, coupled with his angelic-sounding name, inspired in me. "Gabriel Guirlande," he added, his face softening a little, his black brows quirking above his hypnotic stare.

"It was my mother's intention to tell you about me," I said. "In case you don't already know, I'm Benjamin Blackhurst's granddaughter."

"Benjamin Blackhurst is dead," he said, confirming what the cab driver had already told me.

"I know," I said.

"Is that why you've come to Blackhurst? Because you imagine he might have remembered you in his will?"

I gave him an appalled stare. "I'm sorry if that's what you think about me," I said haughtily. "Now, if you don't mind, I want to see my mother. She's waiting for me."

I stooped to gather up my bags, setting off determinedly beneath their cumbersome weight along the oyster-shell drive.

I had gone only a few steps when the house became visible, its pillars rising ghostlike at the far end of the pecan alley. In the half-light the house appeared to be lost behind veil upon veil of shadow, the shrubs and vines crowding around it seeming somehow soft and sinister, like the sluggish black streams that laced through the surrounding cane fields, filled, my mother had once told me, with malevolent quagmires.

Giant live oaks thrust up out of the overgrown gardens, their moss-draped limbs reaching like thickly gnarled arms to guard the antebellum mansion, the decorative balustrades of a second-floor gallery faintly visible through the funereal strands. Pale blossoms drooped from thick clinging vines, swaying gently in the rising wind to form an exotic screen against the backdrop of moving shadows. Behind the vines, something . . . someone moved.

Briefly, so briefly that I could not be certain afterward that I had seen anything at all, I glimpsed a face, scarcely more than a pale oval framed by the rustling greenery.

Then whoever had been there, peering out at me from the west wing gallery, was gone.

Where was my mother I wondered. Was it her face I had glimpsed staring stealthily out from behind the thick greenery to watch for me?

The foliage of parkinsonias brushed against me as I picked my way along the narrow path to the house leaving behind the green-vaulted drive. The first huge drops of rain splashed onto the worn bricks at my feet. No welcoming gleam of light shone behind the mansion's darkly glittering panes; no one stirred in the terrible stillness behind the tall windows.

A footstep scraped across the brick pavement behind me, and I whirled nervously about to find Gabe Guirlande watching me, his bronzed features lost to me in the dimness of the gallery.

"There's nothing here for you, Tracey O'Toole," he said softly. I caught the white flash of his teeth, saw the gleam in his dark eyes that seemed suddenly to burn at me with some palpably threatening fire. "Nothing at all."

Chapter FOUR

I moved away from Gabe Guirlande toward the door, prompted by something I had seen behind his eyes to reach for the heavy knob without knocking. Hesitating only slightly, I gave it a sharp turn, pushing the door inward to step boldly through the wide opening into the murky dimness of Blackhurst Hall.

Gabe stood in silence behind me, waiting.

I knew, without being able to see their shadowed doorways, that a series of spacious rooms were arranged at either side of the seventy-foot-long great hall. Most of the rooms, my mother had once told me, opened onto the deep, shadowy galleries which overlooked the jungle growth of gardens left untended for so long that they were dark even at midday.

Now it seemed that the nameless shadows which had moved before me as I hurried along the pecan alley had preceded me into the house to linger in the dark corners, lying murkily across cypress-plank floors strewn with mellowed Aubusson rugs and Persian runners.

I must have shuddered beneath the force of that intangible onslaught, for behind me Gabe Guirlande said, "My car is parked around back. I'll drive you back to the city. You can take a room there for the night and catch an early-morning flight back to the Coast."

"As I told you before, I've come here to be with my mother, who is ill and needs me," I said coldly, his domineering presence alarming me more than I was willing to admit, least of all to myself.

For it seemed increasingly apparent that Gabe Guirlande had his own reasons for attempting to spirit me away from Blackhurst Hall, even before I could make my presence known to my sick mother, who would never have sent for me had her need for me not been urgent.

"You aren't fooling me, you know," he said, his teeth gleaming between lips that curled to mock me. "Surely you are capable of finding a more convincing reason than the one you've given me to explain your sudden appearance here."

"Are you trying to tell me my mother isn't ill after all?" I demanded. "Or that if she was, she has since recovered sufficiently to return to San Francisco?" I

49

added, a note of desperation entering my voice when it occurred to me for the first time that something like that was entirely possible.

I had been unable to reach the plantation by telephone to tell my mother that I would be on the first flight I could book.

Nor had I stopped to consider the length of time involved between the time she had posted her letter and the time it had eventually reached me, relayed to me by Mrs. Costain who might very well have kept it in her possession longer than she had been willing to tell me. There had been a further delay of nearly twenty-four hours between the time Mrs. Costain had handed the letter to me and the time my flight left San Francisco. It was not inconceivable that my mother might have in the meanwhile caught a flight going in the opposite direction.

But that did very little to explain why Gabe Guirlande did not seem to know that my mother had been summoned to Blackhurst Hall to help Seena nurse my ailing grandfather in the first place. Particularly if Gabe had himself spent a considerable amount of time closeted with my grandfather in his sickroom, as my mother's letter had said.

Surely she could not have told me that, had she not met Gabe Guirlande and herself been made aware of his relationship to my grandfather. It was inconceivable for her to have assisted Seena with her nursing duties without having had some personal contact with any others who had access to the dying man's sickroom. Knowing my mother as I did, it was easy for me to presume that she had taken it upon herself to see to it that her father's waning strength was not overly taxed by his conferences with his attorney.

Why then did Gabe Guirlande want me to believe that my mother was not, nor had ever been at Blackhurst Hall?

I stared at him through the shadows, attempting to read his expression, more unnerved than ever by the failure of my aunt or anyone else in this house to come to my rescue. What if it should happen that there was no one here at the moment, no one but myself and Gabe Guirlande, whose persistence in asking me to leave seemed in itself to pose some kind of threat to my well-being?

He said, when I continued to watch him, "You're serious, aren't you? You actually believe there is someone here named Lorainne, wasn't it? Lorainne O'Toole. But I assure you you're wrong about that. I've

51

no idea where your mother has got to. I only know that she isn't here at Blackhurst Hall, whatever she may have told you. As it happens, I'm in a position to know. I've spent a good deal of time out here during the past few weeks, sitting beside Benjamin Blackhurst's sickbed."

"As his attorney, I understand," I said, wanting him to know that my mother had kept me informed.

"My presence seemed to give him some comfort," Gabe countered. "He had come to be like a father to me."

"There's no way I could have known about you if my mother hadn't told me," I said, attempting to ignore the queer, crawling sensation of fear moving along my spine.

Turning away from his watchful stare, I called bravely, "Is anyone at home? Mother? Anybody?"

The mansion's empty silence echoed around me, flinging my words back at me as though in mockery.

Where were they, I wondered on a wave of growing desperation. Where was my mother? Or, in the event she *had* caught a flight back to San Francisco before I could reach her, where was my Aunt Seena and the half-Cajun cousins my father had spoken of in a voice edged with an indefinable disdain? Surely there was someone somewhere to lend me some familial support in the face of Gabe Guirlande's statement that my mother was not here nor had ever been; someone who could refute his words for me while, at the same time, letting him know that he was not nearly so cognizant of what occurred in this house as he imagined himself to be.

As my eyes became accustomed to the gloom of the house, which was intensified by the gathering storm, I made out a winding staircase curving upwards at one side of the broad hallway. It twined around a central well where an ancient iron-grilled elevator hung, suspended from a precarious arrangement of frayed ropes and ornately wrought pulleys. A woman stood on the stairs, her face scarcely more than a pale blur in the half-light.

I found myself wondering how long my mother's sister had been standing there watching us.

"Your Aunt Seena," Gabe said to me in a soft voice, so low that it seemed almost to be conspiratorial.

She was a small woman, her pale hands fluttering like white moths above the curving, satiny wood of the banister.

"Gabe?" Her voice was like my mother's, softly affected, flowing down to us like honey. "That is you, isn't it, darling? You're back so soon. I do hope you located the trouble with the lines." Then, for the first time, she seemed to notice me. "I see you've brought someone back with you. A young lady, isn't it?" It occurred to me that she was nearsighted even before she reached for the harlequin glasses which dangled from a chain about her neck, perching the frames briefly on the bridge of her nose — a nose that, my mother had once told me, my aunt had always hated — to give me a perfunctory look.

"She's stunning," she said to Gabe, as if she imagined me to be deaf. "Magda will be rabid, of course."

Magda. Gabe Guirlande was committed in some way, then I caught myself thinking, wondering at the same time who Magda was. One of my cousins, perhaps?

"Seena, this is Tracey," Gabe said, as my aunt started toward us down the stairs, her jeweled spectacles resting again between breasts which were still shapely, their rounded contours visible beneath draped layers of clinging green chiffon.

I knew from the questioning look that came onto Seena's face that she had failed to recognize my name.

I said, that same cold, creeping sensation of fear that had come over me earlier taking hold of me again, "Your niece, Aunt Seena. Tracey O'Toole."

As pale as her face was — its milky whiteness carefully preserved from the ravages of the sweltering Louisiana sun beneath upswept hair that was a perennial shade of red — I saw her blanch. At the same time, her hand flew up to clutch at the slender column of her throat and the fiery green stone in the ring she wore flashed at me like a wicked eye.

"Tracey? Lorainne's daughter?" Her voice was scarcely more than a shocked whisper. "But of course. I see it now. You're quite like her." Almost at once her tone had altered, taking on a frosty edge of disapproval.

But not before I realized that she had not been expecting me; that, like Gabe Guirlande, she viewed my presence here as an unpleasant intrusion.

Taking my arm, Gabe drew me toward her along the wide hallway, his tense fingers biting into my flesh, as though I were a common thief he had caught trespassing and it was his intention to escort me off the family property.

I would not be treated like this. Not in my grandfather's house.

Pulling sharply away from him, I demanded of Seena, "My mother? How is she?"

"What is this?" Seena stared incredulously into my face, something that might have been fear flickering behind her eyes. "Why are you asking me this? How do you expect me to know how she is? It's been years since I last heard from Lorainne. We haven't been in touch since she came here to attend your grandmother's funeral. That was . . . how many years ago? A half-dozen at least."

I gave her an appalled stare, wondering if my ears were deceiving me.

When I had found my voice again, I said, "But she came here in response to the letter you sent to tell her that my grandfather was seriously ill."

"I've no idea what Lorainne has told you," Seena said, watching me suspiciously. "But the truth is, she chose simply to ignore the letter I sent. The least she could have done was to send me a note saying she couldn't come. But apparently that was expecting too much of her." Seena's voice was underscored with a seething bitterness that left me stunned.

It was a moment or two before I could collect my shattered thoughts enough to answer her.

When at last I spoke, my own voice sounded harsh and accusing. "Why? Why are you doing this to me? Surely you don't still resent my mother so much that you would try to keep us apart when she needs me?"

"You know then that Lorainne and I never got on well together," Seena stated. "Actually, that is something of an understatement. The truth is, I despised what she tried to do to me. There's a difference, you know, between condemning someone's behavior and disliking her as a person. And after all, Lorainne is my sister, regardless of the fact that she once tried to steal my husband away from me."

"But my mother would never do anything like that," I protested, suddenly aware that Gabe was watching me with a look that had become slightly pitying.

"It happened before you were born," Seena said matter-of-factly.

I did not know how to answer her, wondering if it was possible that what she had told me about my mother and Ves Verret were true.

It was Gabe who broke the uneasy si-

57

lence, saying in a voice that had become surprisingly gentle, "Don't you think it might be best if you left now?"

I answered him with a stunned shake of my head, able then to say to Seena, "I've always known there was friction between you and my mother. But that's not enough reason for you to do this to me now. You must know how anxious I am about her. And she wants to see me. Please take me to her, Seena. Now." I added with a coldness that surprised me. "Otherwise, I shall search this house until I find her."

"You'll do nothing of the sort," Seena snapped, her voice edged unmistakably with alarm.

What was my aunt trying to keep hidden from me? *What had she done to my mother?* The thought crept unbidden into my mind, filling me with a sudden dread.

No doubt this will dismay you, but it has been decided that I shall remain here at Blackhurst Hall indefinitely, my mother had said to me in her letter.

I wondered now, as I had done when I first read my mother's message, whether Seena's bitterness against my mother was so great that she might have tried, in some devious way, to harm her? My heart thudded with a sudden panic which threatened to send it into my throat, when I realized how little I actually knew about my aunt and her offspring, none of whom I had ever met. *A quartet of savages,* my father had said of my half-Cajun cousins. Had he meant to imply that they were capable of treachery?

I had no way of knowing that now.

At the same time, it remained painfully evident to me that Seena did not welcome my presence here. For the first time, I realized how alone and vulnerable I was, here in this house that was isolated from its neighbors by miles of cane fields and cypress swamps with their eerily rising mists and treacherous quagmires. There was one quagmire in particular which was more dreadful than any of the others, my mother had once told me. Known as *The Devil's Well,* it had long since become scarcely more than a legend. Nevertheless it was said to have devoured any number of unwary souls who had been foolish enough to wander alone into the marshes during the mansion's early history. In those times it served as an effective threat, held over the heads of any slaves who proved to be recalcitrant.

As if he had seen into my thoughts, Gabe reached to take my arm, his touch burning into my flesh. "Come along, Tracey."

Again I shook my head, pulling away from him to face Seena. "I shan't let you do this to my mother and me," I said. "I've as much right to be in this house as you do, and I shan't leave here until I've found her."

"Tracey, darling," Seena's voice was pained. "Surely Lorainne hasn't made me out to be the ogre you seem to imagine me to be. We had our differences, true. But to cause you to think of me as a heartless witch of some sort . . . Particularly when I was the one who was wronged."

Very deftly she had succeeded in putting me on the defensive.

I said, "What am I supposed to think when I have a letter written in my mother's own hand, sent to me from Blackhurst Hall, telling me that she has fallen ill in this house and needs me?" I opened my purse, my fingers searching feverishly for the letters I had intended to bring with me.

The letters weren't there, and it occurred to me then that in my haste to reach my sick mother's bedside, I must have left them in the inside pocket of my tote bag where I had put them for safekeeping after the robber's attack on me.

"Well?" Seena watched me expectantly.

"I must have forgotten to bring them," I said awkwardly.

"Them?"

"There were two letters from her, both of them sent from here," I said.

"They can't have been too important, can they, if you've forgotten them," Seena commented.

"My only thought was to reach her as quickly as possible," I said.

"In any case, perhaps you can remember enough of what the letters said to give me some idea why you seem to persist in the belief that your mother is here at Blackhurst Hall."

Briefly I told Seena what my mother had written, mentioning her intention to speak to Gabe but leaving out the part about the lines from Fuller's *Life of Monica.*

A grim look hardened Seena's small, irregular features. "Whatever Lorainne may have said to you in the letters you claim to have had from her, she had no right to involve any of us here at Blackhurst Hall in her little scheme," she stated. She looked at Gabe, something that might have been suspicion darting behind her eyes that were a queer, pale shade of green. "Lorainne hasn't been in touch with you behind my back, has she?" she demanded to know.

"I haven't been contacted by her," Gabe said diplomatically.

Seena shot me a triumphant look. "You see, Tracey. She is up to something."

I had endured enough of this. I wanted to shout out to both of them that my mother was not the kind of person who was in the habit of amusing herself by inventing crafty games.

I said coldly, "I don't know what you are talking about."

"But it's obvious, isn't it?" Seena said. "Your mother wanted you to *think* she was here at Blackhurst Hall, for reasons of her own that we can only surmise. Evidently she went to a great deal of trouble to make her letters sound convincing. Although anyone in St. Bridges could have told her that Gabe was Father's attorney. And she already knew that your grandfather was desperately ill, from the letter I sent her asking if she could come here to help me care for him. Don't you see, darling? She's used my request as a convenient excuse to get away . . ." Her voice trailed off, while at the same time her brows rose in a suggestive gesture, leaving me to make what I would of her cruel analysis of my mother's motives.

Plainly she wanted to believe — and to have me believe — that my mother was keeping some dark secret from me, something indiscreet, perhaps even scandalous.

I said, "My mother and I have always been close. If there were some private reason why she had wanted to get away for awhile, she would simply have told me."

"How long has it been since your father died?" Seena asked. "A year? Two years? Lorainne sent us a formal little note at the time to let us know she'd been widowed. Surely you can't be so naive, Tracey, as to expect a woman like Lorainne to stay true to her dead husband's memory." The bitterness had entered her voice once again, turning it to acid.

"If she had gone off with a man, I'd have known," I stated.

"Would you?" Seena asked softly. Her penciled brows rose suggestively above her pale eyes.

Suddenly I was no longer certain. Soft, gentle, loving, my mother was a woman who needed looking after. It had been partly for that reason that I had abandoned my plan to attend business school in favor of doing modeling jobs for Guy Lannin and other photographers. I had become painfully aware of her vulnerability following the death of my father, quietly assuming responsibility for both of our lives when I realized that, of the two of us, I was the stronger.

"In any case, I want you to know that you're welcome to stay here with us for as long as you want," Seena was saying in that same soft voice, as though my mother's defection were an established fact that served to create a bond between us.

I was unprepared for her abrupt about-face, following as it did in the wake of her shocked reaction when I had threatened to search through the numerous rooms of the house until I had succeeded in locating my missing mother. It occurred to me then to wonder what manner of game Seena herself was playing.

But because there was no other real choice left to me, considering the contents of my mother's letters, I said, "If you don't mind. I should like to stay here at Blackhurst Hall for awhile. At least until I have succeeded in finding her."

Seena watched me for a moment or two, as if it were her intention to challenge me again. But apparently she thought better of it. For she turned then to lead the way up the broadly curving stairs, sliding into the role of gracious hostess with an ease which made me more wary of her than ever. It seemed then that she exuded a soft, cloying charm, made tangible by the heavy scent she wore, and it reached to surround me, as though she were determined in some indefinable way to bring me under her spell.

Or was it the gardens I smelled, the aroma of heavy blossoms mingling with the scent of molding humus seeping into the house, wrapping itself around me like the funereal smell of a death wreath?

So intense was the impression I had of death and decay, that I started when Gabe said behind me, "I'll bring your bags up for you, if you're certain this is what you want."

"I'm certain," I said, glancing at him across my shoulder.

He smiled, his lips crooking cynically below eyes that continued to mock me. "Is any of this worth it?" he asked softly.

I did not need to ask to know what he was thinking: That I was a fortune hunter who had arrived here under false pretenses, hoping to claim a share of my dead grandfather's estate. That, or he knew a great deal more about my missing mother than he was willing to have me guess.

Suddenly the shadows of the house

seemed to weave themselves around me like those long-ago spider webs which had decorated the gardens for that first bride's wedding. I had the uncanny sensation as I slowly began to climb the stairs that, even had I wanted to leave Blackhurst Hall, it was already too late for me to tear myself free from the threads which seemed to bind me to this place as surely as if they had been iron slave chains.

Chapter FIVE

My familiarity with the house resulting from the descriptions my mother had given me as a child served only to increase the discomfort I felt as Gabe guided me upward in Seena's wake, past handpainted wallpaper panels, long since faded, whose scenes presented charming panoramas of men and women in Georgian dress sauntering through palatial gardens.

The broad risers curved gracefully around the deep, central well where the wrought-iron elevator hung suspended inside an ornate framework.

"Ladies and gentlemen seated on the elevator's varnished benches were pulled upward to survey the Blackhurst acres from the promenade which surrounds the mansion's belvedere. The elevator was powered by half-a-dozen stout slaves, who manned the complicated network of ropes and pulleys," my mother had said of the ancient lift.

Lost in the childish fantasies I had conjured around the old house, I had never considered that, should I ever view the lift for myself, it would appear so ominously hazardous.

As if she had sensed my unease, Seena said, "Perhaps I should warn you that the elevator is no longer in use. Years ago, one of the ropes snapped, and a guest here was paralyzed for life by the fall, her back broken. Of course it has been repaired since then, and an electric motor installed. But I can't remember the last time anyone dared to set foot inside it."

"Whoever was hired to install the motor neglected to replace the ropes with wire cables," Gabe contributed. "Things like ropes have a habit of deteriorating rather badly in this humid climate."

I remembered the frayed pull which hung down from the old slave bell mounted beside the gate. "I'll keep that in mind," I said, for the last thing I intended was to attempt to transport myself between the high-ceilinged floors by means of the dilapidated contraption sagging inside the gracefully twining curves of the polished-cypress handrail.

We had arrived at the second-floor landing. The staircase continued to spiral above us to the third-floor landing and the glassed-in belvedere on the mansion's mansard roof, which commanded an unobstructed view of the surrounding countryside. Gabe followed with my bags as Seena led me swiftly along a broad hallway which branched at its far end to penetrate the wings I had earlier glimpsed behind obscuring layers of vines.

A door opened as we passed by, and the light from the sconces mounted beside it fell softly across the tawny features of a dark, slender woman in her late twenties, whose kohl-rimmed eyes regarded me with a curious hostility.

My first impression when I saw the brightly patterned scarf tied so low across her forehead that it touched against her black brows was of a gypsy.

"Magda!" It seemed to me that Seena flinched beneath her fierce stare. "I had no idea you'd returned so soon from your ride. Darling, this is your cousin Tracey, Lorainne's daughter. Surely you remember my sister, Lorainne O'Toole," Seena added nervously when the woman poised in the doorway failed to respond.

Instead, Magda shifted her stare to Gabe, raising a slim brown hand to tuck the tip of the slender black cigar that smoldered between her fingers into a mouth that might have been beautiful had it not been for the cruel twist of her lips. "Where did you find her?" she asked when she had taken a long, slow draw on the villainous cigar, allowing the smoke to sift between her lips in small, gray wisps as she spoke. "Or was it she who found you?"

"I can't see that it really matters, one way or another," Gabe said. "The point is, your cousin is here now. The least you can do is to make her welcome."

For a moment or two, Magda continued to challenge him with her stare, standing with her black-booted feet apart, the cigar held tensely to her lips. A gold serpent ring crawled up one finger to the knuckle, its soft glitter reflected in the tangle of gold chains draped around her neck.

Deliberately she shifted her gaze to me.

"Tracey." Her sullenly drooping mouth quirked into a dazzling smile that came as a surprise, coupled as it was with the fierce black gleam of her eyes. "I must say, you don't look the part. But, then, appearances can quite often be misleading, can't they?" I did not miss the note of mockery in her voice, hearing something false and contradictory in her that I wanted to back away from.

Instead I said, watching her face closely for some signal which would tell me that my mother had been here more recently than either Gabe or Seena wanted me to know, "If you mean that I fail to resemble Lorainne, I've been told that I do."

But if I had hoped to detect a betraying flash of recognition behind her dark stare, I was disappointed. Instead, what I saw was malice.

"I was referring to your lack of resemblance to a vulture," Magda said in saccharine tones. "That *is* why you've come, isn't it? To scavenge whatever you can from Grandfather's estate?"

I stared numbly at her, rendered speechless by the unwarranted viciousness of her attack.

It was Seena who spoke, her voice rueful, "Tracey has some misguided notion that Lorainne is here at Blackhurst Hall. I've told her that we've not seen Lorainne in years. Not since your grandmother passed away. But I have a distinct feeling that she doesn't believe me."

Magda flashed me a disdaining look. "What kind of schoolgirl's prank is this? Or do you imagine all of us here to be fools? I for one refuse to be taken in by your little ruse."

Angry frustration welled up in me, causing my cheeks to flame. "Think what you want of me," I said. "All I am interested in at the moment is finding my mother, who happens to be missing."

"According to Tracey, Lorainne has managed to implicate us in whatever mischief she's become involved in," Seena said, sounding suddenly weary.

"In what way?" Magda's fierce stare flashed between us.

"My mother wrote to me after she arrived here in response to Seena's request that she come help attend to the needs of my grandfather," I repeated for my cousin's benefit, watching her face again for some sign which would serve to give them all away.

Again there was nothing beyond the obvious dislike she felt for me, which seemed to me to be completely unjustified, considering that the two of us had never met before in our lives.

"I trust you've brought her letters with you." Magda's manner was frankly challenging.

"Unfortunately Tracey forgot to put them in when she packed her bags," Seena said, before I could find words to defend myself. "However, according to what your cousin has just told Gabe and me, Lorainne is here somewhere in the vicinity of St. Bridges. Or was. I've invited Tracey to stay with us here at Blackhurst Hall for as long as it takes to find her."

"Whatever you say, Mother." It seemed to me then that Magda's mocking tones held a note of warning which was directed in an offhanded way at me, although I could not be certain, surrounded as I felt myself to be by hidden undercurrents of hostility and suspicion.

Nor did I miss the look Magda darted at Gabe, as the three of us started off again down the long hallway, Seena leading the way with hurrying footsteps, as though she were as eager as I to escape Magda's intimidating comments. Magda's boldly illuminated eyes had both scorned and commanded him, burning with their own bright passions behind the languorous trails of smoke curling upward from the fiery tip of the hideous black cigar she had thrust again between her lips.

A quartet of savages. The words my father had used to describe my cousins flashed once more across my mind. Gabe, too, was a Cajun, I reminded myself, recalling Seena's remark which had seemed to suggest that he was in some way committed to Magda. Were the two of them engaged to be married, I caught myself wondering. In which case, I thought quickly, they would make a striking couple, with their tawny coloring and expressive black eyes.

At the same time, I could not deny my own awareness of Gabe Guirlande. His personal magnetism compelled me in a way I neither understood nor wanted. The result was that I found myself wanting nothing so much as to escape to some quiet place where I could be alone with my own tumultuous thoughts.

Seena paused to open a door a short distance from where the hallway branched toward the wings.

"I think you'll be comfortable here," she said, standing aside to show me into a spacious room filled with eerie contrasts of darkness and light, as the storm sent jags of lightning across the barely visible sky beyond the deep overhang of the gallery.

A queer sense of nostalgia swept over me as I realized that the room to which Seena had brought me had once belonged to my mother.

Seena's next words confirmed what I already knew. "It was your mother's room when she was a girl," she said. "She had a passion for old things, pieces that I'd have tossed out long ago if we could have afforded better. I hope you won't find it too depressing."

"I'll be close by should you happen to need me for anything," Gabe said, putting my bags on the bed. His words might have been intended for either of us.

I waited for him to go before I said to Seena, "I hoped you'd put me in this room."

"Lorainne told you about us, then." Seena touched a switch beside the door.

The room stayed as it was, shrouded in gloom.

"Damn," she muttered beneath her breath, trying the switch again. But to no avail. "The storm must have blown a fuse," she said.

Her face was scarcely more than a pale blur in that queer, aqueous light, as she toyed with the ineffectual light switch.

"There's no telephone either," I said. "I tried to reach my mother at this number several times during the past week, and again shortly before my plane took off, to let her know I was coming."

"It would have saved you a great deal of trouble if you could have gotten through to us," Seena remarked. "Unfortunately we've had problems with the line recently. Gabe was out checking it this evening to see if something might be done about it before this storm hit us. You never know what emergency might arise. It's a little frightening to be out of touch at a time like this. But not nearly so bad as being without lights."

I became aware of wind whipping with a sudden savagery around the third-story dormers, splashing monstrous drops of rain onto the wildly swaying greenery beyond the darkly sheltered gallery. There was the soft, ghostly clacking of tree limbs knocking together and a louder sound as a branch tore loose and came crashing down onto the roof of the veranda.

I gave an involuntary little shudder, watching Seena go to lift the round globe from a Sevres china hurricane lamp which stood on the table beside the canopied bed.

"Rosewood furnishings by Prudence Mallard and François Signouret of New Orleans," I commented, more to break the tense stillness of the room which was punctuated only by the storm outside, than to show that I knew.

"Straight out of a mausoleum," Seena remarked, opening a drawer to search for matches; then, when she failed to find them, going to look in a chest across the room. "What else did Lorainne tell you about us?" she asked across her shoulder.

"Surely she wasn't content to limit herself to some drab inventory of the Blackhurst antiques." Although her voice was casual, I caught a note of something that might have been fear, perhaps even dread, behind it.

I said carefully, "She spoke of being a girl in this room."

"As monstrous as they are, these pieces have become rather valuable." Seena had found matches somewhere, and, ripping one of them from the small book she held in her hand, she came toward me, striking it with a vicious little jab across the sanded strip at the matchbook's base. "But of course you know that." The flame leapt to illuminate her pale eyes when she bent to hold it to the wick of the Sevres lamp, whose base was hand-painted in a pattern of full-blown yellow roses, repeating the ornamental tracery of the bulbous globe.

The oil-soaked wick sprouted a tapering flame, the thready orange banner rising to illuminate Seena's flawless features. For a stunning instant, I saw guilt plainly written on my aunt's face, coupled with the fear that had been mirrored by her voice, and I wondered again what she was hiding in this house that she did not want me to find.

Suddenly I could no longer contain my own dark sense of dread, and I found myself turning nervously about to search the room's dim corners for some small bit of evidence which might betray my mother's presence here. My mistrust of both Gabe and Seena had been intensified by the encounter with Magda.

I saw the pale gleam of Sevres and Dresden lamps and vases, and I was aware of gold-framed mirrors reflecting gleaming rosewood and mahogany, a marble-topped side-table, and the faint patterns of a faded Aubusson carpet. But if I had hoped to find a lost earring glittering up at me from out of the pale pools of light that spilled across the floor, or perhaps a forgotten scarf tossed carelessly above the bed's fluted mahogany posts, its colors blending so subtly with the Italian brocade hangings that it may have gone unnoticed, I was disappointed.

The room was devoid of any sign of recent occupancy, the bare tops of the rosewood dressers and chests gleaming coldly in the yellow lamplight that should have lent a warm coziness to the mellowed woods, but that instead seemed only to emphasize their barrenness of any single item which might have proved to me that my mother had been here.

The room itself showed care. I caught the gleam of polished glass through the ancient ecru lace curtains which veiled the tall French windows; nor was there any hint of dust clinging to the deep swags of ruby velvet draped above the fragile panels, although their gold tassels had become tarnished. But that was to be expected, I thought. The pierced plasterwork of the dentilled cornices was cracked in several places, and there was a chip in the onyx cap which topped the verde marble fireplace.

As though the chipped mantel might provide me with the clue I sought, I went to run my finger absently across it, wondering if the other rooms in this huge old house were as immaculately kept as this one. Or was my mother's old room the exception? And if so, why? I was not so naive as to imagine that Seena might have had it looked after out of some lingering sentimentality.

"A Yankee soldier did that." Seena's voice cut across my thoughts. I looked around quickly to find her watching me from beside the bed, her slim hands tugging nervously at the voluminous mosquito *barre,* as though, I thought, she had needed an excuse to remain with me to see what I would do. "The story has it that some long-lost cousin of yours ridiculed him when he became amorous. In his rage and frustration, he struck out at that priceless piece of onyx."

"He must have had a terribly fragile ego," I commented, feeling slightly repelled.

"He was the enemy," Seena stated, something in her tone alerting me. "Your ancestress had the good sense to shoot him before he could damage it further."

I gave her an appalled stare.

"What would you have done, Tracey, had you woken to find the enemy hovering over you while you slept? She had no choice but to kill him. Fortunately her father had given her one of his dueling pistols to keep in her bedside drawer in the event it became necessary for her to protect her virtue while he was away fighting the Federals. It's still there, incidentally. But of course it will no longer fire after all these years."

I had the uncomfortable feeling that Seena had told me the story as a warning.

"What happened to my ancestress after she had killed him?" I could not resist asking, thinking that I had been right about this house with its seething under-currents of evil and tragedy; thinking, too, that my mother had severely edited any tales she had seen fit to tell about the mansion's history.

"She, along with her mother and older sisters, was clever. As are all Blackhurst women," Seena added in all seriousness. "They turned the house into a club of sorts for the Union *officers*." I did not miss my aunt's emphasis. "It was to their own best interests to give the generals and their aides the best sherry there was to be found in the Blackhurst cellars, while the daughters of the house entertained them with their accomplishments on the piano. Of course the neighbors all turned on them. But they loved this house and would have done anything to save it. They had the foresight to hide all of the finest silver at the bottom of the cistern, and the choicest pieces of furniture were carried up to the attic. General Nathaniel Banks himself was assigned to the most lavishly appointed of all of the mansion's guest rooms, the same room that was later used by his Confederate rival." Seena paused. "But I mustn't wear you out with my tiresome prattle about what's been over and done with for years. Goodness knows Valmir will do enough of that, should you give him half a chance."

"Valmir?" I remembered the list of Verret family names my father had recited for me, knowing even before Seena spoke that he was my cousin.

"Your only male cousin," she clarified. "He's only just returned from a visit to Baton Rouge where he spent all of his time digging around in the State Library in an attempt to verify some of the old stories about this place." Seena gave the room a cursory glance. "Now if you're sure you'll be all right here, I'll go see what Henri is attempting to do about the lights." Seena went to the door, turning when she had opened it to face me. "I forgot to ask if you've eaten."

I shook my head. "It doesn't matter. I'm really not hungry."

Seena brushed my words aside with a flutter of her pale hand. "Nonsense. I'll send Odalie up with a tray. Henri and Odalie have been with us for years, ever since your mother and I were girls. They'll both be curious about you. Meanwhile, I suggest you get out of those hot travel clothes and soak in a tepid tub. There will be time enough for you to meet Valmir and his sister, Valerie, in the morning. Particularly since I haven't the least idea where those two have gone off to. And in this weather . . ." She left me with a fond shake of her head which seemed to suggest that, of my quartet of savage cousins, the two she had named were her favorites.

Chapter SIX

I rushed to open drawers when Seena had gone, prying shamelessly into their corners with my fingers. If my mother had been here at Blackhurst Hall at some point during the weeks since she had been gone, surely she had left behind some small, betraying bit of evidence to prove her presence.

The dueling pistol lay in the drawer of the bedside stand, just as Seena had told me. I went next to the towering armoire which stood between the French windows. There were empty hangers inside the huge wardrobe, arranged neatly beneath a shelf which contained a stack of cast-off candy boxes, their faded ribbons suggesting that they had not been disturbed in years. Not since my mother had inhabited this room as a girl, I thought. Had they been gifts to her from her suitors? I had never before considered my mother in that context — as a pretty, perhaps even frivolous, young woman, pursued by a flock of amorous admirers. Now it seemed to me that the candy boxes with their expensive padded covers and faded ties presented a side of her that I had not suspected was there, and I found myself wondering if what Seena had told me could possibly be true. Had my mother attempted to steal her own sister's husband away from her?

The last thing I wanted to believe of my mother was that she might once have become involved with her own brother-in-law. At the same time, I remembered that my father had had small use for Ves Verret. It occurred to me now that his remarks labeling my Cajun uncle an idler and a wastrel had been oddly out of character. Now that I had been confronted by Seena's bitter accusations against my mother, his comments seemed suddenly to confirm my aunt's worst suspicions about her, particularly when I recalled my mother's grim-lipped refusal to respond to the unflattering observations my father had made concerning her brother-in-law's lack of responsibility and ambition.

Still, I could not believe that my mother had gone off on her own, whether alone or with someone, as Seena obviously wanted me to believe. Not without first explaining to me where she was going and why. Nor did it seem reasonable to assume that she might have attempted to mislead me by pretending to be at Blackhurst Hall, while in fact, if Gabe Guirlande and Seena were to be believed, she had never been here at all.

If that were true, why would she have written to tell me that she was taken ill, at the same time urging me to come to her as quickly as possible? In the event that Seena was right about her and she had come to St. Bridges to keep a secret rendezvous with someone I knew nothing about, surely she would have told me where she was, if nothing else. Otherwise how could I be expected to find her?

I remembered that, according to her letter, it had been her intention to tell Gabe Guirlande about me, and I wondered now if it were possible that she had intended for him to direct me to her. If so, why had he failed to comply with her wishes?

My mistrust of the handsome attorney grew when I considered the frightening possibility that even now my mother might be lying ill somewhere, perhaps in some dingy hotel room, patiently awaiting my arrival. Or had she been too ill in the first place to carry out her intention of letting him know I was coming?

My mind continued to whirl in a wild

confusion of chilling thoughts and conjectures, none of which seemed to be even remotely logical when I stopped to consider how close my mother and I had always been to one another. I tried then to think of what I must do, knowing only that I had no real choice but to remain at Blackhurst Hall until I had succeeded in unraveling the mystery that seemed to surround her strange disappearance.

Unexpectedly the electricity flashed on, lighting dressing table lamps at either side of a gold-framed mirror. Giving up my fruitless search, at least for the moment, I blew out the oil lamp and, taking my robe and pajamas from my bag, I went with them into the adjoining bath where a huge marble tub crouched on tarnished brass feet, its waterspout shaped to resemble a long-necked swan.

There were gardenia-scented bath crystals in a cut-glass container on the marble counter beside the sink. Turning on the water in the tub, I spilled the green crystals beneath the pouring spout and slipped out of my clothes, sliding gratefully beneath the fragrant water as the tub filled.

A sound in the adjoining room alerted me to the fact that I had been soaking in the tub long enough and, imagining that what I had heard was Odalie arriving with the tray Seena had promised to send up to me, I quickly toweled myself dry and put on my pajamas and robe.

There was no one there when I returned to the room which had belonged once to my mother. More puzzling still, the room was shrouded again in darkness.

Assuming then that Odalie had snapped off the lights as she left, leaving the tray for me to find, I moved cautiously in the direction of the switch beside the door. It was then that I heard it: The soft click of a latch, as though someone had been standing outside in the hallway, peering in at me past a door held slightly ajar.

Moving forward on a sudden impulse, I grasped the door's ornate knob, swinging the heavy panels abruptly inward and stepping quickly into the hall outside. The feeble glow from the acanthus-leaf bracket lamps cast myriad restless shadows along the hall's vast length, reflecting dimly in the polished woods of the furniture groupings arranged at intervals along the papered walls.

Briefly, so briefly that I could not be certain that I had seen anything at all, I glimpsed movement beyond the dark turn where the hallway branched to enter the west wing, several yards beyond the point where I stood. In that same startling instant, I was reminded of the pale face I had seen earlier, peering down at me from behind the tightly laced vines which draped the west wing gallery. Had there been someone there after all; someone who had slipped along the dimly lighted corridor to enter my room while I soaked in the huge old tub?

Uncomfortable without knowing what it was that made me uneasy, I turned back toward the darkened room, reaching to touch the switch beside the door. But to no avail. The room around me remained shrouded in darkness, and I realized then that the lights I had left burning in the adjoining bath had gone out as well, as had the wall brackets in the hall outside.

There seemed to be nothing then for me to do but to light the oil lamp again and, feeling my way carefully past a tall chest whose polished wood felt cool and satiny to my touch, I went in the direction of the chipped mantel where I had seen Seena put the book of matches before she left.

The sound of rain dripping off foliage came to me from beyond the tall windows and I realized that the storm had diminished while I had my bath, for I could hear above the wind the bullfrogs in some nearby swamp.

Somewhere an owl hooted. I stopped to listen for an answering call, as something my mother had once told me rose from the depths of my memory to hover uneasily on the surface of my mind: *A lone owl is bad luck. If you hear a single hoot, there's nothing left for you to do but to turn around and go back the way you came.*

The colorful superstition had been a part of the Negro lore she had absorbed as a child, growing up here in this rambling old house, with its haunting memories of a way of life which had long since vanished. But it was a way of life that had left an indelible imprint on any who had ever lived here, I thought, when I recalled the stories she had told me about the mansion.

Determined to return my mind to more practical matters, I walked quickly to the fireplace and ran my fingers swiftly along the top of the mantel. The matches I had expected to find there were gone.

Next I ran the flat of my palm down the full length of the polished onyx. But it was no use. If Seena had put the book of matches there, as I was certain I had seen her do, whoever had entered my room while I lay in the tub had taken the matches with them.

It seemed that unless I wished to spend the remainder of the evening shrouded in darkness, I had no choice but to try to find Seena to ask her for more matches. That, or wait for Odalie to appear with my tray.

Deciding then that the easiest way was to wait for Odalie who, if Seena were true to her word, should be arriving shortly, particularly since I had not the least idea which of the mansion's many rooms belonged to Seena, I went to the canopied bed. Parting the fragile folds of the mosquito *barre,* I slid between them onto the brocaded spread.

Pulling the folds of my robe tightly around me in a protective gesture, I lay back wearily against the thick pillows. Something cold and evil probed into my cheek and I sprang up with a startled cry.

At precisely that same moment, the lights flashed on again, so that I found myself thinking sometime later that it was entirely possible that the brief blackout had been prearranged.

For now, however, the thing on the bed commanded my full attention. Brief as my first glimpse of it had been, I had no trouble recognizing the dueling pistol that distant cousin of mine whom Seena had told me about earlier had used to shoot the Union soldier who had dared to invade her boudoir. It lay with its viciously notched muzzle pointing directly at the spot where only seconds before my head had rested.

The pistol's presence on my pillow had a paralyzing impact on my already shattered senses. For a stunned moment or two, I could only stand there staring down at it, chillingly aware that someone had entered my room while I lay soaking in the big tub; someone who had removed the pistol from the drawer to put it where I would be sure to see it.

Numbly it occurred to me that so far only three people knew of my arrival: Gabe, Seena, and my cousin Magda. Which of the three had entered my room to place the pistol on my pillow in such a threatening gesture? Gabe? Was he even more determined to have me leave here than I had first imagined?

Or was it Seena who wanted to frighten me? I had no illusions about my aunt's feelings toward me. It was obvious that she blamed me in some remote way for the grievances she thought my mother had been the cause of. It made little difference whether or not Seena's resentment of her younger sister had any real basis in fact. The frightening thing was that my aunt seemed thoroughly to believe that my mother had wronged her, in a way which had left Seena twisted and bitter in her attitudes toward us both.

Magda? Was it she I had glimpsed, disappearing beyond the dark turn in the hallway when I had rushed to swing open the door?

Not that it really mattered which was responsible for placing the gun on my pillow, I thought. I did not need the name of that person to know that whoever it was had intended the dueling pistol to serve as a warning. Its evil implication was unmistakable: If I persisted in my decision to remain at Blackhurst Hall — in spite of the fact that Seena had invited me to stay — I was placing my life in jeopardy.

Lifting the gun gingerly between fingers that had begun to tremble, I replaced it carefully in the nightstand, slamming the drawer quickly closed as though by putting it out of my sight, I could banish its sinister implications from my mind.

But it was not to be that easy.

My appetite, which had been nonexistent to begin with, had turned to a dull, sick feeling when, at last Odalie arrived with my tray.

"I'm sorry I've put you to so much trouble," I told her, glancing with genuine regret at the fluffy omelet and golden triangles of buttered toast she placed on a low table before a ruby-brocaded settee at one side of the fireplace.

A waxy magnolia blossom, still damp from the rain, quivered in a corner of the tray, and there was strong hot coffee in a silver pot, its aroma failing nevertheless to tempt me.

"It's no bother, Miss Tracey." Odalie, who proved to be a tall, gaunt woman, her yellow skin suggesting that she was more white than black, watched me in silence for a moment or two, her black eyes frankly assessing me. "You the spittin' image of your mama when she was a girl," she finally said. "How is Miss Lorainne, child, been so long since I last saw her."

Been so long . . . I realized on a sudden wave of despair that I had been counting on Odalie to help me, although it was not clear, even in my own mind, what it was that I had expected her to do for me. Tell me that my mother was in this house, in spite of Seena's fervent denial of her presence here? That did not seem likely, considering that Seena was her mistress. Nor could I be certain that all of them, including Odalie and her husband Henri, were not working against me for reasons which I had yet to discover.

I said, watching Odalie's glossy face closely, "How long has it been since my mother was here last?"

She gave me a curious stare, as though, I thought, she were questioning my sanity. "Why surely you know that as well as I do, honey," she finally said. "You must have been ten or twelve at the time. Seems like Miss Lorainne told me how old you was when I asked about you while she was with us. All I know is it's been too long. Way too long." Her voice that was low and husky had hardened with something that might have been disapproval.

"Why is that?" I asked as casually as I could.

"Your grandpapa's dearest wish was to lay eyes on her one last time before he died," Odalie said. "Least she could have done was to come see him, even if it was for just a little while."

Purposefully, she went to turn down the bed, her gesture telling me as clearly as if she had spoken her thoughts aloud that she intended to say no more on the subject of my mother's failure to attend to what Odalie obviously considered a daughter's sacred duty. But what puzzled me most was my own certainty that my mother had felt precisely as Odalie did, her eagerness to reach my grandfather's bedside when Seena had sent for her taking priority over everything, including myself.

Absorbed by my own bewildering thoughts, I could only pick at the food Odalie had brought me.

"Fixing for you, Miss Tracey, is like giving a fish a drink of water," the housekeeper grumbled when she turned away from the bed to find the omelet still untouched. "Or is it that you don't like what I've brought you? Like I tell Miss Magda, just because you like roses ain't any reason to despise the sunflower," she added testily.

"It's fine," I said. "It's just that I'm not hungry."

"My turn to ask why," Odalie said, bracing her hands on lean hips encased in faded cotton print to regard me with an assertive authority. "It's all right to tell me what's bothering you, child," she prompted. "I been looking after the folks in this house since before your mother was in didies."

I regarded her for a moment or two in silence, wondering how much I dared to reveal to her concerning my reason for being here. How far could I trust any of them in this house, including the elderly black servant who had once been my mother's nursemaid?

I said cautiously, "My aunt didn't tell you why I've come?"

"She said something about a lost cause, if that's what you mean."

A lost cause . . . Had the hooting owl been right then? Was I defeated, even before I had begun, in my search for my missing mother? All things considered, was I being foolish not to turn around to go back the way I had come?

Suddenly I felt hot tears welling behind my eyes. Brushing them angrily away, I said, "My mother is supposed to be here, in this house."

"Why you saying a thing like that to me, Miss Tracey?" Something that I identified as fear flashed behind Odalie's *café-au-lait* features. "I already told you Miss Lorainne ain't been here since the Old Missus died and was carried off to be buried in the graveyard out behind the old sugar house." She hesitated. Then, coming to lay a moist palm gingerly across my forehead, she said, "You sure you feeling all right, child? The

97

way you talking, I'm beginning to wonder if maybe you ain't fevered."

"I'm just tired is all," I said wearily, logic telling me that if my mother were here at Blackhurst Hall, lying ill in one of the vine-shadowed rooms, surely Odalie, of all people, would be aware of her presence, if only because it would be necessary for someone to prepare her meals for her.

I watched with sagging spirits as the elderly housekeeper gathered up her tray to go, a dreadful thought tugging with a wearying persistence at the edges of my mind: What if, when my mother had arrived, whoever had put the dueling pistol on my pillow had used some similar method of coercion in an effort to drive her away? What if she had chosen to ignore that chilling threat in her eagerness to help Seena attend their dying father during those last dismal days of his life?

She had arrived in St. Bridges by bus late in the evening nearly a month ago, that much I knew from the phone call I had received from her. I also knew that she had been waiting for one of my cousins to pick her up and drive her here to Blackhurst Hall. Yet of those I had so far encountered in this house, none would profess to having seen her.

In which case, was it possible that she had met with foul play before whichever one of my four cousins she had been waiting for could reach her? I was able to put that particular theory promptly to rest when I remembered the letters I had received from her three weeks after she had called me.

None of it seemed to make any sense. Not unless someone here had coerced her before the others had had a chance to see her. The thought sent a fresh wave of dread through me when my vivid imagination conjured a picture of her hiding from one of them even now, in some dismal little room in St. Bridges, waiting for me to find her.

However, in spite of my apparent ability to visualize the worst, that particular theory did not satisfy me either. For even though something like that might have occurred, there was still no reason why in her letters she should not have told me where she was.

Wherever she had disappeared to and for whatever reason, I could not forget that it had been her intention to tell Gabe Guirlande that she had sent for me. Nor could I put from my mind the fierce way he had looked at me when I had come upon him in the pecan alley. The barbaric method he had used to dispose of the evil-looking little snake that had slithered into my path left no doubt in my mind that he was a man capable of cruelty, perhaps even murder.

At the same time, I remembered the remark he had made to me describing his relationship to my grandfather. Like father and son, he had said, as though, I thought, he imagined himself to be entitled to some special consideration as a result of that friendship. His suspicion of my own motives, coupled with his interest in Magda, seemed to confirm my own growing suspicion that he felt himself to be entitled to some portion of my grandfather's estate. I had no idea what provision had been made for its disposal. Nor did it particularly interest me, in spite of what those who lived in this house wanted to believe were my reasons for coming here.

But that did not explain where my mother had gone to, nor did it tell me why Gabe Guirlande had been so determined to take me away from Blackhurst Hall even before I could make my presence known to the aunt and cousins I had never met before tonight.

The only thing that seemed clear to me

at the moment was my own certain knowledge that I must remain at Blackhurst Hall
for as long as it took for me to find my
mother, regardless of the threatening gun
someone had arranged on my pillow.

Apart from that, nothing else mattered.

Chapter SEVEN

When I went down the following morning to breakfast, I found the others gathered around a wrought-iron garden table in the courtyard behind the house.

I did not need to ask to know that the darkly handsome man and stunning, black-haired girl were my half-Cajun cousins, Valmir and Valerie. The table sat beneath a rose-choked trellis, and small pools of sunlight spilt down through the freshly washed leaves and blossoms to gild their glossy, dark heads and sun-browned faces.

They did not see me at first as I came toward them on the path from the gallery steps to the sheltered niche beneath the roses. Or if they did, they did not show it by glancing in my direction.

Pausing for a moment or two, I watched them, thinking how incredibly alike they were. Twins, I thought, somewhat younger than Magda, who sat opposite them next to Gabe's place at the head of the table. Seena sat across from Gabe, her red hair immaculately coiffed even at this early hour. But her face looked tired and strained, as though, I thought, she had slept very little, if at all.

As I continued to watch, I was aware of an air of conspiracy in their manner. They were the ones who belonged in this house, not I. Apparently it made no real difference that I was as much a Blackhurst as any of them. I was the outsider who had intruded here, stepping into their lives unannounced.

I went toward them, the giant elephant ears beside the path rustling wetly against my legs.

"Here you are at last, Tracey," Seena said, when I entered the fragrant bower. She motioned for me to sit in the vacant chair next to Magda. "We were just talking about you, dear," she went on with a false brightness. "These are your cousins, Valmir and Valerie. I've already told them who you are."

A quartet of savages . . . I wanted to ask her where my fourth cousin was, but instead I nodded shyly across the table at the clannish pair, who regarded me curiously. The mottled sunlight shifted across their faces so that it was impossible for me to read what they were thinking. Perhaps for that very reason, it seemed that I saw something oddly sly and wary in their tanned faces, as though they were merely a reflection of one another, each of them serving to mirror the other's thoughts and impressions. Twins, I thought more certainly this time, almost identical save for the difference in sex.

Valmir was the first to respond to my quiet acknowledgment, his lean face breaking suddenly into a dazzling smile that instantly dispelled the impression I'd had of a foxlike stealth lurking within. I was able then to tell myself that it had been some unfortunate mingling of light and shadow when I had first looked at him that had caused me to see something in his face that I had not liked.

"Tracey." He continued to charm me with his smile. "Seena was just telling us you've come here hoping to find that Lorainne had arrived to pay us a little visit." His voice contained the barest hint of sympathy. "I'm sorry that we can't produce her for you. I can imagine how concerned you must be, having her go off this way with no warning of what her true intentions might be."

His words alerted me, putting me instantly on the defensive.

I said indignantly, "My mother is not in the habit of misleading people, least of all her own daughter."

Valmir's face brightened with an intensified interest, my challenge obviously exciting him. "I should have been disappointed in you if you hadn't stood up for her," he said. "If there's one thing I admire in a woman, it's loyalty to her own causes."

"What else *could* she say, under the circumstances?" Valerie remarked, her tone deprecating, while managing at the same time to patronize me.

"None of us has any way of knowing what another will do, given the right circumstances," Seena said vaguely. "Anyone is capable of anything when the conditions are right. After all, we are all of us only human, including my sister."

"You are in a position to know, Mother," Magda said in her drawling way, turning to flash me a mocking little smile. "We're all aware that Lorainne once tried to steal that wild Cajun father of mine away from Seena," she went on knowingly.

"I can't believe anything like that ever happened." My voice was more angry than I meant it to be. "And even if it did, what has it to do with now? Especially since Ves Verret has been dead for years."

"We all know how distraught you are," Seena said, giving me a look that, although it was lacking in sympathy, was nonetheless tolerant. "Since Gabe has finally managed to locate and repair the break in the phone line, I suggest that you call San Francisco when we've finished breakfast to see whether or not Lorainne may have turned up there. It's quite possible that she has returned home by now and is wondering where you are. I'm certain this whole thing is just one of those unfortunate mixups that sometimes happen to people. A lack of communication, as they say."

It was more painfully obvious to me than ever that no one here was prepared to take my concern over my mother's disappearance too seriously, influenced as apparently they all were by Seena's prejudices against her.

More frightened and frustrated than I wanted them to know, I said, "I suppose you could be right," wondering even as I spoke if I dared to grasp at so feeble a straw.

My lack of conviction must have sounded in my voice, for Gabe said with a hint of compassion that I had not expected him to show, "It won't hurt to try there. As Seena said, it's impossible for anyone to second-guess another person's motives. No doubt there is some perfectly logical explanation behind your mother's failure to tell you for certain where she'd be."

But I know my mother, I wanted to shout at them all. The notion that she was involved in some secret endeavor of her own was absurd. Yet, what if it were so?

But I would not think about that. No matter where my mother was or what she was doing, she would find a way to contact me if she were able, that much I knew.

If she were able . . . The thought lingered chillingly in my mind. She had told me in her letter that she was ill. Was it possible that she had been stricken so suddenly that she had been taken to a hospital, in lieu of coming here to Blackhurst Hall?

I became aware of Valerie, her face sullen as she watched me.

"Don't look so tragic, Tracey," she said. "It's not the end of the world, you know. There are ways to find out where she's gone, if it should come to that." There was something slyly secretive behind her sullen smile; something that frightened me a little.

"I had hoped it wouldn't be necessary to go to the police," I said uneasily.

"That could prove to be embarrassing

for us all," Seena said.

"I had something else in mind," Valerie stated.

"But I don't understand," I said, staring into her narrow, heart-shaped face.

I was acutely aware of the contrasts that were in her, as she continued to watch me for a moment or two, whether for effect or because she was not quite certain that she wished to confide in me, I could not tell. It was as though something dark and hidden lurked behind a face that she had deliberately attempted to brighten by an application of some fragrant oil to her smooth tawny skin.

The result was a subtle, golden shimmer highlighting her forehead, cheekbones, and chin. But she could not disguise the dark brooding I saw in her eyes, as though, like the old house looming out of the greenery behind us, she was filled with her own bleak and haunting shadows.

Was it Valmir who had this devastating effect on her? I wondered curiously. Was she the dark side of the coin to his light?

"Don't be so mysterious," Magda said crossly when Valerie continued to watch me in that queer, brooding way.

"I was thinking that a charm lamp might help," Valerie finally said. "That is, if you believe in such things. Do you, Tracey?"

"I haven't the least idea what a charm lamp is," I told her.

"It happens to be Valerie's version of lighting candles to the Virgin," Valmir said before she could explain for herself what she had meant to imply. "I may as well tell you now, Valerie has some strange notions. You'll do well not to take any of them too seriously. Meanwhile, I'm volunteering to serve as your own private genie. And you needn't light a candle to conjure me either. If you want me for anything — anything at all — just call my name and I'll come running." He flashed me a flirtatious smile, the sun-browned skin at the corners of his eyes crinkling so that I could not be certain whether he meant his words as a mockery for Valerie, or as a message for me to take seriously.

In any case, Valerie was not pleased with him. I saw anger flash behind her eyes, turning her small face stormy.

"Valmir brave him, who drinks two pots of *café noir comme le Diable* that is strong, strong, yes, before he goes out to wrestle alligators in the swamp. Yes? Yes!" She spoke in what even I recognized as a stereotyped Cajun patois, the conflicting emotions I saw smoldering behind her forced smile betraying themselves in the slightly quavering timbre of her voice.

"As you can see, some of us here aren't entirely civilized," Magda said to me in her drawling voice, pausing to take from the gold case beside her plate one of the slender black cigars she affected. Fitting the cigar into an ornate holder, she sucked in her smooth cheeks when Gabe leaned to light it for her. "Valerie considers Valmir her own private property and always will, I suppose," she remarked, a spiral of blue smoke curling from between her brightly painted lips as she spoke. "God pity the woman who tries one day to steal him away from her."

If I had expected Valerie to deny her possessiveness of Valmir, that was not to be the case.

Instead she said, her black eyes seeming to warn me, "We Cajuns are a clannish lot."

Surprisingly it was Valmir who protested. "I can almost feel *Grandpère* turning over in his grave," he said, adding apparently for my benefit, "He loathed anything that wasn't strictly apple-pie American."

"He was terribly fond of Gabe, you know that," Magda said.

Valmir gave me one of his engaging smiles. "What Magda is trying to say is that *Grandpère* approved of Gabe's initiative and ambition, in spite of his involvement with the French language renaissance and his coincidental attempts to rejuvenate the deflated Cajun pride."

I said awkwardly, "I gather that our grandfather was a man of strong opinions."

"He was a stubborn old bastard," Valmir stated. "He could never quite bring himself to admit that he cared two whits for any one of us, if only because of what our father was." There was bitterness in his voice, whether for my grandfather or Ves Verret I could not tell.

Magda flashed me a look. "You know of course that Ves Verret was a full-blooded Cajun. Just as Gabe is," she added significantly.

I glanced helplessly at Seena who appeared to be overwhelmed by her wild offspring, her pale face vague behind the jeweled frames of her glasses as she pretended to become absorbed in one of the newspapers I had seen inside the mailbox the previous evening.

Behind my aunt's indifferent pose, I sensed a tense wariness, even fear.

"I suppose you like to think of yourself

as Evangeline," Valerie was saying bitingly to Magda. "Although I'm quite certain she didn't go about smoking those stinking cigars you've become so addicted to. Nor can I picture her striding about as if she owned the whole world, lashing out with some hideous blacksnake at anyone who dared to oppose her."

I noticed for the first time the ivory handle of an evil-looking whip lying beside me beneath the table, on Magda's lap, its long black thong coiled like the snake for which it was named.

The disbelief I felt, coupled with a sudden revulsion, must have shown in my face, for Magda said, "Does my friend frighten you, *couzan?*"

"I've never seen one of those before is all," I said as calmly as I could.

"I doubt if Evangeline did, either," Valerie persisted.

"Evangeline was a loser," Magda retorted.

Vaguely I recalled the epic tale of the Acadian girl who had spent the better part of her life searching for her lover, only to learn when she eventually found him that he was married. It was with a small sense of shock that I remembered his name had been Gabriel, my gaze going against my will to Gabe Guirlande's handsome Cajun face.

Briefly our gazes locked and I felt the fire rising to my cheeks when he said in an amused voice, "I don't want to disillusion you, Tracey. But the Cajun version of that old tale has it that Gabriel was not only married when Evangeline finally caught up to him but that he also had three mistresses and thirteen children."

I tried desperately to find a retort for him that would not sound girlishly gauche and naive. I was relieved when nothing came to me to see Odalie approaching us along the overgrown path, her narrow shoulders sagging beneath the weight of a burdened tray.

I became aware of a luxury and extravagance I had not expected to find here, as Odalie moved about the table to serve us, lifting the protective covers from steaming platters of ham and eggs and a plate of hot sliced biscuits smothered in real butter. There were monogrammed jelly dishes containing quivering mounds of *mespilus* and muscadine preserves and a fresh pot of coffee strong enough to stain our cups, in addition to the traditional grits, which I had never tasted before.

I remembered my father's infrequent references to the hardships my grandparents had been forced to endure as a result of

Seena's widowhood, wondering for the first time if it was possible that he'd had something other than financial deprivation in mind. The food Odalie set before us was of the finest quality, the china from which we ate priceless.

My first impression when I had arrived at the mansion the previous evening had been of gross neglect and decay.

Now it seemed suddenly that the acres of unkempt gardens with their darkly shielding shrubs and vines served only as a deliberate guise behind which Seena and her brood sought to hide from the outside world. The effect was strengthened when I remembered the locked gates which had seemed so formidable to me, in view of the taxi driver's ill-disguised skepticism when I had told him where I was bound. Nor could I forget his eagerness to escape back to town, leaving me alone in the shadow of the old slave bell.

In any case, the state of the family coffers was no real concern of mine, I told myself now, allowing Seena to refill my cup with *café noir* from the ornate silver urn Odalie had replenished from the steaming pot before she gathered up her tray to go.

Turning to Gabe, who was spreading the pale yellow preserves on one of Odalie's tender biscuits, I said, "Was Valmir serious? Are you really involved with the revival of the French language in Louisiana?"

"Here." He reached in front of Magda to hand the biscuit to me. "I doubt if you have wild plums in San Francisco. Besides, you're not eating." His gaze commanded me to accept his offering and taste it, which I did, caught off guard as I was.

"I was never more deeply involved with anything in any life," he said. "With one or two possible exceptions," he added, the seriousness of his demeanor belying the lightness of his voice.

There were contradictions in him that eluded me, and I found myself wondering if all Cajuns were as obscurely complex as both he and my cousins appeared to be.

I said, brushing crumbs from my fingers, "But are there enough people of Cajun ancestry here to make it really worth your while?"

"There are nearly a million-and-a-half French-speaking people in the state, the majority of them Cajuns," he said, pride edging his voice.

"But if your people already speak French, what is there for you to do?" I asked.

"They may speak a passable version of their mother language, but very few of them can either read or write it effectively," he told me.

"In other words, they are an illiterate lot of backward crayfish men, like my father," Valmir said.

There was no mistaking this time whom the bitterness in his voice was directed against, and it occurred to me with a small sense of shock that, for all of his Cajun clannishness, Valmir Verret had hated his father.

"You are bound to catch a glimpse of at least a few of them while you're here, rowing about the swamps in their crude pirogues like ignorant savages," he went on in that same acid tone.

"You were far too young when your father died to remember what he was like," Seena protested.

It was Magda who said, in a voice shot through with some darkly seething emotion of her own, "Ves Verret was fierce, the kind of man whose name becomes legendary."

" 'Captains and conquerors leave a little dust, and kings a dubious legend of their reign.' " Gabe quoted softly, lifting his cup to regard me across its delicately gilded rim. "I suppose that's better than being forgotten altogether."

I did not know the lines he had recited. Nor did Magda appear to recognize them, her look questioning him, becoming slightly suspicious.

My only thought then was that, like my mother, Gabe Guirlande was familiar with poetry. It was a side to him I had not expected to find and one that further piqued my curiosity when I remembered that it had been my mother's intention to tell him about me. Had she seen a side to him that she had imagined she could trust, because of his ability to quote the muse? And if so, then what?

Once more I had allowed my questing thoughts to lead me into treacherous territory.

I said, looking carefully at Gabe, as if to find some clue in his face that would tell me the truth about where my mother had gone, "Are those lines supposed to mean that Cajuns are like gypsies, with a hereditary ruler of their own?"

"Nothing quite so romantic as that," he said. "Although I must confess we're clannish. More clannish than most, I would imagine."

"This is the twentieth century, for God's

sake," Valmir protested, grimacing with distaste. "You make us sound as though we've only just recently emerged from our caves."

"Valmir's problem is that he's never quite been able to measure up to his paternal heritage," Magda said. "Ves Verret was a free soul, afraid of nothing. His feats of bravery are legendary up and down the bayous. While Valmir, poor dear, is clever at absolutely nothing, unless it's his ability to spend money we don't have in pursuit of his own foolish pleasures."

"The *last* thing I want is to emulate my father's primitive passion for blood," Valmir said heatedly. "I prefer to see myself as a respectable planter, in the best Blackhurst tradition."

"And you shall, darling," Seena said, glancing up from her paper. She gave me a strained little smile. "Your cousins were more your grandfather's children than his grandchildren. He was the only real father they ever knew. Now that he's gone, Gabe has been helping us with whatever decisions are necessary and to make certain the hands do their jobs properly. Although, of course, Valmir shall assume full control of the plantation in time. It's merely a matter of familiarizing himself with the

118

way things operate. Your grandfather was not a man to relinquish the reins easily, even after he had become far too ill to make any kind of rational decision of his own."

"I don't want to disappoint you, Mother," Valmir said, "but it's not my intention to become merely an overseer." As pleasant as his tone was, his implication was unmistakable: If Gabe Guirlande was content to ride into the fields to check on the hands, he was not.

Sitting there in all of his sun-browned splendor, Valmir, I knew, had not acquired his tan by any ordinary means. Both he and Valerie exuded a languid air of luxury, in their matching silk shirts and exquisitely tailored, flare-bottom pants.

It was Gabe who wore boots and jeans. Gabe, and Magda, with her wickedly coiled whip and smoldering black cigars.

I did not know what to make of any of them, including my aunt, who was saying to Valmir in a coaxing voice, "As the man of the family, you are going to have to expect to be at least partially responsible."

"I intend to be fully responsible," Valmir stated. "The problem is, Seena, that you have cast me in an inferior role. I have no more intention of emulating Grandfather than I do Ves Verret, slaving like some ignorant field hand in this damnable sun until my brains are fried. Small wonder Benjamin Blackhurst wasn't in his right mind when he died."

"I had no idea Grandfather was . . . *non compos mentis*." I glanced at Gabe. "That is the term they use, isn't it?"

He nodded, his face grim. "It's a term that covers a wide range of infirmities," he said.

"Don't allow yourself to be misled by Gabe's glib legal jargon," Valerie said. "The truth is, the old man was crazy. Mad as a hatter."

"That's putting it rather strongly, isn't it, dear?" Seena's expression was pained, and I thought again that she was intimidated by my cousins, seeming almost afraid, as though they held some invisible power over her.

Pulling her gaze quickly away from Valerie's sullen face, Seena said to me, "The doctors called it a little stroke. It wasn't as though he had become . . . insane." Her voice had fallen to scarcely more than a whisper, her narrow shoulders quaking in a little shudder.

I found myself wondering then what my grandfather's true condition had been.

Had he become violent, perhaps even dangerous? Did that explain why Gabe Guirlande had spent so much time closeted with him in his sickroom, as my mother had told me in her letter?

Or did the very fact that my mother had failed to mention to me that my grandfather had become mentally incompetent mean that she had never been here at all? And if so, where was she?

The barrage of uneasy questions her strange disappearance had given rise to seemed endless, filling me with a sudden, dark despair when I realized that I had not the least idea where to begin my search for the answers I needed if I was ever to find her.

Chapter EIGHT

I called San Francisco, as Seena had suggested, when I had finished with breakfast. When there was no answer, I dialed the hospital in St. Bridges, only to discover that no one there had ever heard of Lorainne Monica O'Toole.

Because I had hoped so desperately that my mother would answer and my fears would be instantly dissipated, that first moment after I hung up the receiver was filled with an overwhelming disappointment.

Turning away from the phone, which was mounted in the ground-floor hallway, I hurried out through the mansion's front doors to lose myself in the gardens.

I did not hear Magda's step until she was upon me, the inevitable cigar smoldering between the fingers of her left hand, the ivory-handled whip I had seen coiled in her lap at breakfast looped loosely around her other palm.

"I wondered where you had sneaked off to," she said accusingly.

"Is there any particular reason why I shouldn't come and go as I please while I'm here?" I asked, recalling Seena's quick response when I had threatened, upon my arrival, to search the mansion's numerous rooms for some sign of my mother.

Now I realized how foolishly I had behaved if my impulsive response of the previous evening meant that I was to be watched while I was here, as Magda's critical attitude seemed to suggest.

"That depends," she finally said in response to my question.

"On what?" I demanded to know.

"On where you take it upon yourself to go and whom you choose to go with," she said.

"Are you threatening me?" I challenged.

Magda shook her head slowly, her manner openly mocking me. "No, *couzan*. I don't make threats, me."

I stayed where I was, refusing to be intimidated by her feigned Cajun ways.

Glancing at the whip that dangled casually between her fingers, I said, "Then why must you carry that thing about with you, as though it were your pet snake or something?"

"Does it make you nervous, *couzan?*" she asked in her low drawl.

I shook my head quickly. Too quickly.

"Would you like me to show you how Ves Verret used it to protect his authority?" she asked in that same low voice that seemed in itself to pose some kind of threat to my own well-being.

"I've never cared for violence," I said as casually as I could, hoping that by pretending a disinterest I was far from feeling I could discourage a display I did not want to see, no matter how clever she imagined herself to be.

"The whip is the least violent weapon I can imagine. In the hands of an expert," she added, tucking her cigar between strong white teeth to toy with the thin black thong, allowing it to slide sinuously between her fingers, caressing it, I thought, as though it were a live thing she had become overly attached to.

"Really, I don't care to see you demonstrate," I said.

"This is a woman's weapon compared to the knife my father used," Magda said, her fascination with the snaking black leather beginning to alarm me a little. Was she perhaps a little mad? I found myself wondering about that when she continued to fondle the slithering coils. "His best feats were won with the bowie knife," she went on. "It's customary in the Verret family for the ruling male to stake out his claim whenever he enters the house of a *couzan* by plunging his blade to its hilt in the center of the table. More than once, as a child, I watched Ves Verret split a table in half with his skill and his strength."

"I find that barbaric," I said, more shocked than I wanted to be when I remembered that this was the man Seena had accused my mother of attempting to steal away from her.

"Lorainne found it fascinating," Magda said uncannily, as if she had seen into my mind to read my appalled thoughts.

"I don't have to listen to this," I said, spinning away from her knowing stare to strike off along a moldy side path, half-expecting to feel the biting sting of her whip across my defenseless shoulders.

I had gone only a few paces when something small and dark and slimy shot before me across the broken bricks. My nerves already on edge, I came to a jarring halt, giving a startled little cry.

In the next instant, Magda's whip slashed past my ear with a shrill, whistling sound that caused the hairs on my neck to prickle. A long green tail flicked and I glimpsed beady eyes staring vacantly up at me out of a tiny severed head. So swiftly had my cousin struck that it was a moment or two before I realized that the creature lying dead at my feet had been nothing more than a small harmless lizard, its red air bladder slowly sagging as its slender body separated to writhe away from me in an opposite direction.

More sickened now than afraid, I spun to face my cousin.

"Murderer!" I shrilled at her in a voice edged with hysteria. "How could you be so heartless?"

Briefly she stared at me, her black eyes glittering with a strange, dark excitement. Then, without saying a word to me, she turned and stalked away, the ugly black-snake coiled once more around her palm.

More shaken by the encounter than I wanted to admit to myself, I fled toward the rear of the house, striking off between banks of pale yellow acacias and pink crepe myrtle trees. Finding myself on an over-grown walk leading in the direction of the old kitchen and the overseer's office, which stood nearby on the far side of a narrow, lily-choked pool, I remembered that it was here in the old office that my grandfather had kept his plantation records. Always his favorite, my mother had come here often as a child, to lose herself in her volumes of poetry while my grandfather sat before his big rolltop desk, attempting to balance his books.

Now, although it was not my intention to go snooping about where I had no real right to be, I found myself going toward the office doorway, pausing before I stepped onto the thick cypress plank which crossed the pool, to make certain Magda had not turned again to follow me. There was no sign of my cousin in the midst of the thick gardens, although I could not be entirely certain that she was not hiding somewhere to spy on me.

As uneasy as that particular thought made me, I continued on toward the office, stepping gingerly onto the deep veranda which ran the full length across its front.

Pausing once more behind the wall of vines which transformed the long gallery into an aqueous green tunnel, I peered out between the heavy fronds, searching again for some betraying movement which would tell me that Magda was watching. But if she had turned to follow me along the sheltered path, she was nowhere to be seen.

Still half-expecting her to materialize out of the nearby greenery in an effort to forestall me, I went nervously to try the office door. Even as it occurred to me that the building might very well be locked, the knob twisted easily beneath my fingers, the door swinging smoothly inward on hinges that had been recently oiled. Stepping swiftly inside, I closed the peeling panels quickly behind me.

Surrounded as it was by shrubs and vines, the building was dark inside. Staying where I was for a moment or two, my back pressed tensely against the doorjamb, I waited for my vision to adjust to the verdant gloom seeping in through dusty windows shrouded in cobwebs.

Gradually I was able to make out a Brumby jumbo rocker standing near the foot of a steep dark stairwell, its woven cane seat and back tattered by time. The rolltop desk that I had known would be here stood between the tall dingy windows opposite a yawning fireplace. Peeling posters and fly-specked calendars decorated walls that had turned brown with age, and there were cardboard boxes and odd sticks of furniture stacked carelessly into a dark corner beside the boxed-in staircase.

But all of my attention was for my grandfather's desk. On its top, between recumbent Bennington stags in matching flint enamel, stood a pedestal-base oil lamp. An antler on one of the stags was chipped, and I guessed that the priceless set had been a gift to some distant ancestor of mine but that it had since been relegated to the overseer's office, perhaps by Seena, because of the small flaw.

I moved swiftly, lest Magda come looking for me, and find me here where I had no real right to be. With hands that had turned suddenly icy I rolled back the desk's cleverly jointed lid. My first impression was one of careless confusion. Yellowed papers and letters spilled from the rows of deep dark cubbyholes ranged along the back of the desk's spacious interior, and there were several ledgers spread open, one on top of the other, on the ink-stained writing surface.

Feverishly I began to search, not even certain what it was I sought, knowing only that I must begin somewhere to seek an answer which might explain my mother's puzzling disappearance. Methodically, moving from right to left, I rummaged quickly through the contents of the cubbyholes, turning my attention when they failed to yield anything of importance to the large drawers at either side of the cavernous kneehole.

The first drawer I opened contained yet more of the old ledgers, their sturdy cardboard covers printed with a marble pattern. Mildew edged their musty pages that, had they lain undisturbed through the years, would have been pressed tightly together, perhaps even stuck to one another. Yet when I lifted the top ledger from the drawer to glance at the date inside, I found that its pages were loosely ruffled, as though someone had recently found a reason to go through them. My impression then was that someone had searched the desk as I was doing, and I tried to imagine what whoever it may have been had expected to find.

My curiosity triggered, I dug deeper, my fingers encountering a bundle of letters held together by a rubber band. The first name I saw when I withdrew the packet from its hiding place beneath the ledgers was the name of Gabe Guirlande's law firm.

When I saw that the letters were addressed to my dead grandfather, I was more curious than ever. I carried them to one of the tall windows, tugging nervously at the band which held them together. Rotted with age, the rubber band snapped in my fingers and before I could catch them, the letters had fallen haphazardly onto the dusty planks at my feet.

Stooping quickly, I began to reassemble the scattered envelopes, my eyes straining to read the dates of the hand stamped postmarks in an effort to replace them in their original order.

I did not hear his step as he came down the dark stairwell toward me. So intent was I on my task that I did not know there was anyone else inside the gloomy old office until, out of the corner of my eye, I saw the faded legs of his jeans above the tips of his scuffed black boots.

I cowered. The last person I had wanted to find me here, with my grandfather's legal correspondence clutched guiltily between fingers that had begun suddenly to tremble, was Gabriel Guirlande.

For a paralyzing moment or two, he stood over me, his dark gaze accusing me. Then, still without saying anything, he reached to take the scrambled sheaf of letters from me. Going with them to the desk, he laid the letters inside, closing the segmented lid with a carefulness that seemed somehow ominous.

Rising quickly, I tried desperately to think of some logical reason why I should be here, rummaging through my grandfather's personal papers.

But it was no use. I did not know enough about either my grandfather, or his affairs, to know where to begin.

It seemed then that my best defense against this fierce dark Cajun was to pretend a proprietorship I did not have.

I said, when he turned again to face me, "What are you doing here in my grandfather's office?"

"I might ask you the same thing," he countered.

"I'm family and you're not," I shot at him with a false bravado, aware even as I spoke that I was being childish, like a small girl caught with her mother's best lipstick smeared on her party dress.

He continued to regard me in that same grim and quiet way. I had the feeling that somewhere inside himself, he was mocking me, waiting for me to betray myself in some incriminating way.

"Well, why shouldn't I be here?" I blurted when I could no longer bear his discomfiting silence. "I arrive here expecting to find my mother waiting with open arms to greet me, only to discover that she's missing. I happen to know this office was one of her favorite places to come when she was a child."

"Have you found it comforting?" he asked.

Caught off my guard, I said, "I didn't come here to be comforted."

"Obviously." He glanced meaningfully at the desk where he had put the letters he had found me holding. "Which of them told you your grandfather's will was missing?" he asked then. "Seena? Or was it Valmir?"

"I know nothing about a will," I said truthfully.

"Then what *were* you looking for?" he asked skeptically.

"I don't see that it is any concern of yours even if I were searching for something. Which I wasn't," I added, not quite truthfully.

"Seena and your cousins may see it differently," he remarked. "Particularly since they are anxious to find your grandfather's will, which he seems to have misplaced somewhere before he . . . became incompetent," he added, his voice shaded with something that might have been remorse.

I stared curiously into his face. "But surely as his attorney, you have a copy of his will in your possession," I said. "In which case, had I wanted to know anything about it, I should simply have asked you in the first place."

"Unfortunately your grandfather failed to take me into his full confidence as far as the bequeathing of his estate was concerned," Gabe said.

"But I thought the two of you were such good friends," I could not resist saying, a small feeling of satisfaction going through me when I saw him grimace. He was not nearly so impervious as he wanted to pretend, I thought, thinking too that I would not want to be the one who tried to push him too far. I added quickly, "Anyhow, isn't it possible that he might simply have neglected to make one out until it was too late for him to do anything about it? Or perhaps he viewed it as a superfluous formality which he disdained to bother with. After all, Blackhurst Hall has always been ceded to the male heir next in line. It had become something of a family tradition, that much I know from what my mother told me."

"In which case everything would go to Valmir," Gabe said.

"You sound skeptical," I said.

"I have every reason to be. I happen to know that your grandfather intended for it to be otherwise. In any case, even old family traditions require their proper forms and signature, if they are to be legalized. He was as much aware of that fact as I am."

"You sound very sure of yourself," I said, wondering if it were possible that he expected to claim a share of my dead grandfather's holdings in the event that a will could be found.

Was that why he did not want me here? Because he imagined that I might pose some threat to the legality of such a claim?

"I know there was a will, because I witnessed it," he said.

"A holographic will?" I asked, immediately aware, when I saw his eyebrows raise, that I had said the wrong thing.

"I advised him and made suggestions, one of them being that he have a copy of the will made for me to keep for him," he said.

"Apparently you weren't nearly as close to him as you wanted to make me believe," I said, my voice edged with a malice I had not intended.

Too late I realized my mistake, catching the sudden flare of anger behind his eyes even in that murky dimness. He stepped toward me. No, *glided* toward me, his lean body moving with a swift, sinuous grace.

I spun away from him, fear racing like ice water through my veins.

But he was too quick for me.

His arms trapped me, whirling me roughly about to face him. For a shattering moment, he stared at me, his face so near to my own that I felt his breath warm against my cheeks.

I wanted to pull away from him. But there was something in his look that mesmerized me. I knew then that he would kiss me and I let him, conflicting emotions charging so violently through me that I was powerless to resist.

Chapter NINE

Unable to sleep that night, partly because I had arrived absolutely nowhere in my effort to find my mother, partly because I could not put aside the remembered sensation of Gabe Guirlande's mouth burning against my own, I slipped into my robe and went out through the French windows onto the wide gallery to stare moodily into the garden.

Fireflies flashed high in the moss-covered live oaks, seeming to hang like tiny green-white lanterns on the muggy air. Nearer at hand I became aware of the soft, feathery whisper of wings, as a giant moth brushed past my face, flying toward the faint thread of pale light showing between the drawn curtains of my window.

From below, the cloying sweetness of blossoming shrubs rose to wrap itself around me, mingled with the thick smells of mossy walls and damp bricks lost beneath rotting layers of humus, into a heady earthiness that was at once pleasant and perverse.

Lost in my own troubled thoughts, I

moved slowly through pools of black shadow, catching an occasional glimpse of the rising moon through the trees. A spiderweb brushed across my cheek, moist and sticky. *If a spiderweb falls on your face, it's bad luck,* my mother had once told me, repeating another one of the old Negro superstitions that had been a part of her childhood. *It means that your enemies are working their spells against you.*

I wiped the web from my brow with a little shudder. Small rustling sounds rose out of the gardens below me, and from farther away came the soft trilling of a mockingbird. An ominous melancholy seemed suddenly to surround me and I turned back toward my room, realizing that I had come much farther than I had intended. It would be quicker, I thought, to follow the encircling gallery the remainder of the way around the house, thus approaching my room from the opposite direction.

I had arrived at the turn which would take me along that section of the gallery which circumscribed the west wing when I saw her. At first, I imagined that the woman who stood at the far end of the gallery where it turned once more to extend along the west side of the house was my mother.

She was all in white, scarcely more than a pale blur against the backdrop of dark vines that had scaled the thick pillars and festooned the wooden drain troughs at the edges of the roof.

I ran toward her on feet that felt suddenly weightless, calling her name softly.

"Mother?" I called again when she appeared not to hear me. "It's Tracey. I've come to take care of you."

There was a faint fluttering movement, as though she had only just then become aware of my presence, her hand flying to her throat in a familiar gesture. Then suddenly she was gone and there were only the vines, whispering softly beside me as I continued to run, my feet making dull little thudding sounds on the thick floorboards.

I did not see her again until I had turned the corner. Once more she stood at a distance from me, poised at the far turn in the gallery as though she were taunting me.

I grew cautious, assailed by the chilling realization that if the woman who watched me from the gallery's black shadows was indeed my mother as I wanted to believe, she did not know me. What had they done to her?

I started on again, more slowly this time, forcing myself to stay calm as I attempted to reach her. "Mother? Please, it's Tracey. Your daughter, Tracey."

She moved, hovering like a pale moth in the black shadows near the turn. I took a step forward, then another. But I had gone too far. In the next instant, she vanished, as though she had never been there at all.

I ran to where she had been standing, imagining that she had vanished around the corner toward the front of the house, where I had glimpsed a pale face watching me the previous evening as I came up the drive. What strange game was she playing? And why?

Slowing my pace as I neared the turn, I went forward cautiously to peer past the corner of the house.

The long veranda was empty, save for the moving shadows cast by the vines as the breeze stirred there softly. An occasional splash of moonlight penetrated behind the lightly swaying garlands to move along the cypress floorboards like a slowly shifting mirage.

I wondered numbly if it had been only the moonlight I had seen, moving between the tremulous vines in an oddly veiled pattern that resembled a woman clad ethereally in white.

Pressing my forehead against the plastered bricks beside me, I waited for the shattering wave of disappointment that had suddenly assaulted me to subside.

It was then that I heard it. From somewhere nearby came the soft, muffled click of a window latch. I was not going mad after all, I thought wildly. There *had* been someone on the gallery; someone who had cleverly eluded me by slipping quietly through one of the west wing windows.

I moved quickly to pause before the first of the deeply recessed openings. Reaching to explore the seam between the heavy French frames, I became suddenly aware of a small scraping sound coming to me from beyond the panes. In the next instant, my fingers came in contact with the soft, narrow edge of a lace curtain. I realized then what had happened. Whoever the woman in white had been, she had been overly hasty in her eagerness to escape me, with the result that a corner of the curtain had caught between the heavy frames when she had closed the window.

Although my gaze could not penetrate the darkness behind the glittering panes, I knew that she stood nearby, no doubt waiting to see what I would do. Gingerly I tried the windows. If she had not succeeded in pushing the latch all of the way into its receiving slot, she had at least managed to force it enough to secure the thick frames, which refused to budge.

I stood in silence, taking a moment to think what I must do. Was there even a remote possibility that the woman in white had been my mother? Or was it one of the others who stood opposite me now, on the far side of the locked windows? Seena, perhaps, fleeing to hide from me for her own private reasons? Or Magda, up to her wicked tricks again, in an effort to frighten me away from here?

In any case, I had to know.

Pressing my face close to the seam between the thick frames, I called softly, "I know you're there. Please answer me. Tell me who you are."

There was a long, breathless pause. I strained my ears to listen, imagining then that I caught a faint whisper.

"Amber," the lightly whispering voice seemed to say. "Amber."

Amber. That had been the name of that long-ago bride my mother had told me about as a child, I thought vaguely; the bride who had been laid to rest more than a century before, inside the old family vault in the cemetery behind the abandoned sugar house.

I thought then of the beads that the assailant who had attacked me before I left San Francisco had twined so ominously around my neck. Was it possible that whoever was hiding from me behind the west wing's locked windows had slipped into my room during my absence to steal the beads from my overnight case? Did that explain why she sought to elude me? Because she was guilty of theft?

I tried again to imagine which of them it might be. The inaudible whisper had sounded somehow soft and feminine, and it occurred to me then that perhaps it was Valerie, using her own sly methods to discourage me from staying in a house where I was not welcome.

Holding my face close to the locked windows, I said, "If you are trying to tell me that you've taken the amber beads from my bag, I really don't mind that much."

There was a charged silence.

Then the voice on the far side of the windows said, "They're mine! The amber beads belong to me. Someone stole them from my room."

I had not expected this, and it was a moment or two before I could think what to say.

"Who?" I was finally able to ask. "Who

stole your beads from you? Who are you?"

"Amber!" the voice said again. "I don't want you here. Go away, Tracey O'Toole. Go away before it's too late. There's nothing for you here. Nothing at all." The voice had grown louder, its disguised tones hoarse with some barely controlled emotion that penetrated and reached me through the thick wood beside my ear.

Numbly it occurred to me that Gabriel Guirlande had said virtually the same thing to me the previous evening, upon my arrival at Blackhurst Hall. *There's nothing for you here, Tracey O'Toole. Nothing at all.* What did it mean? That Gabe had dressed himself to resemble some ghostly creature in white in his determination to impress those warning words on me? Was it he who stood opposite me even now, clad ridiculously in some castoff from the mansion's attic, his voice disguised in some clever way in an effort to conceal his true identity from me?

But I would not be taken in. Not by Gabe or anyone else.

I said, far more bravely than I felt, "I know who you are." I hesitated, half-expecting whoever was there to challenge me. When no answer came, I went on impulsively, "If you think you can frighten me away from here so easily, Gabe Garland, you are badly mistaken. I won't be taken in by your silly games."

I waited, prepared to bolt away at the least hint of a window beginning to open, when I remembered the kiss he had given me. A kiss, I thought now, that had been merely another of his savage ploys designed to intimidate me.

"No!" the whispering voice finally said. "Amber! Don't you understand? I'm Amber."

Something cold touched me then; something that reeked not of treachery but of madness.

Chapter TEN

It seemed suddenly that I could not escape quickly enough, and I whirled about to run as fast as I could back to the comparative safety of my mother's room.

My first thought when I locked the French windows tightly behind me, untying the gilded cords which secured the heavy velvet portieres to let them fall in thick, smothering folds across the ecru-lace glass panels, was to check my overnight case to see whether or not the amber beads were still where I had left them.

Going quickly to the armoire where I had stored my bags when I had finished unpacking them, I knelt to open the smaller of the two cases, fumbling inside it with fingers that had become suddenly clammy with a dread anticipation.

The beads were there, just as I had left them, lying in a lumpy ridge beneath a torn place in the lining. Reaching a finger into the tear, I succeeded in capturing the slithery strand, drawing the beads out. I carried them to the bedside lamp where I held them against the light and examined them. Was it possible that they might once have belonged to someone in this house? Someone who claimed her name was Amber?

Baffled as I was by my strange encounter with the ghostly figure in white, the insects fossilized inside the transparent amber seemed more sinister than ever, the miniscule appendages attached to their tiny bodies causing them to appear venomously alive inside their tiny resin prisons. I slid the strand slowly between my fingers, drawn to the beads by a dread fascination. The ancestors of today's insects had been much smaller than those with which I was familiar, the flies the size of a modern-day mosquito.

Some of the beads contained mites, and there were miniature moths and cockroaches caught inside the golden droplets. More deadly still, a multi-legged centipede peered out at me from one of the clear beads, its small size enhancing in some queer way the evil it seemed suddenly to embody.

Amber. What had whoever had whispered that name to me from behind the west wing windows meant to imply? Was there someone living there in a part of the house my mother had once told me was no longer in use; someone whom I had yet to meet? Someone named Amber, after that long-ago bride, who did not want me here any more than did the others? I remembered the dueling pistol someone had placed on my pillow. I had imagined then that there were only three persons in this house who had known of my arrival, Gabe, Seena, and Magda. I had failed to take into account the pale face I had glimpsed for the barest instant, watching me from behind the layers of vines which scaled the tapered Tuscan pillars to screen the west wing gallery. Was there madness in this house? Madness which had reached in some macabre way to involve my mother? As dreadful as it was even to contemplate, I could not entirely ignore the possibility that any mother's illness had taken a form which Seena, as her sister, might be determined to keep hidden, even from me. Nor could I forget Seena's strange reaction when Valerie had told me at breakfast that my grandfather had been crazy. *Mad as a hatter.* I had not missed the shiver of dread that had jarred Seena's narrow shoulders, as though the word itself had held some terrifying intonation which she had wanted to shake off.

Surrounded as I sensed myself to be by malevolence and mystery, it seemed then that the amber beads with their ominously trapped insects had begun to scorch my fingers, and I went back to the armoire, searching inside the towering old cupboard for a suitable place to hide them.

My gaze was drawn to the candy boxes stacked on the shelf over my head; their padded covers had long since turned yellow with age. It seemed more apparent to me than ever that the boxes had not been disturbed in years, beyond an occasional superficial dusting. In which case they should serve my purpose, I thought, at least for the time being, until I could decide what to do with the beads that the woman named Amber claimed belonged to her.

Standing on my toes, I reached to balance the edge of the stacked boxes on the tips of my fingers, easing them carefully off the high shelf. I had started to lift them down, my fingers spread to support them like a waiter balancing a precariously laden tray, when a knock sounded on my door.

"Tracey?" The voice belonged to Gabe Guirlande.

Under the circumstances, he was the last person I wanted to see and I stayed where

I was, willing him to go away.

"Tracey?" he called a second time, holding his face close to the closed panels, I thought, to avoid waking the others.

It seemed then that there was something ominous in his quiet tone; something that alarmed me.

Still I waited, half-expecting to see the doorknob turn stealthily beneath his touch, remembering then on a growing wave of panic that I had forgotten to turn the key in the lock.

After what seemed an eon, during which my heart threatened to leap from my mouth, I heard his footfall as he turned to leave. Only then did I dare to relax my arm which still held the tottering stack of candy boxes aloft, suddenly aware of an ache in my cramped muscles.

In the next instant, the pile toppled. The empty boxes crashed down on me with a resounding clatter, sending the string of amber flying from my fingers.

The door to my room flew open. I spun toward it in time to see Gabe enter with a bounding stride, a look that I could not read masking his somber features.

"Tracey, what in God's name!" He stopped abruptly when he saw me standing foolishly in the midst of the boxes. "You should have called Henri to come take those down for you," he said then. "Unless, of course, this is another of your private little search parties." His voice was mocking.

He considered me a meddling outsider, I knew that much from the look he gave me, even before he said in that same softly dangerous voice that I had already come to know so well, "Let it be, Tracey."

"What do you want?" I asked coolly. I became aware of the amber beads lying on the rug near my feet, bending to retrieve them without taking my gaze from his face, slipping them with a swift gliding movement into the pocket of my robe.

His gaze shifted to my fingers. "What is that you have there?" he demanded, coming to draw my hand away from the looped coils which dangled over the edge of the pocket's narrow hem. "Where did you get these?"

His reaction was one of shocked incredulity. Roughly he snatched the beads from me, ripping my pocket with his sudden fierceness when they lodged briefly beneath the fold of the hem.

"Surely you've seen fauna amber before," I said warily, alerted by the expression that had come into his face.

He went without answering to hold the beads against the illuminated globe of the bedside lamp, running them through his fingers as I had done so that the tiny aculeate insects trapped inside seemed to float in the midst of a golden fluorescence.

When at last he bunched the beads in his palm to look at me, his expression was grave.

"Where did you find these?" he demanded.

"I don't see why that's important," I hedged uneasily.

"Surely you know what they are," he said. For once, his voice did not mock me.

"I never saw them before in my life until . . ." I hesitated, Mrs. Costain's description of the man she claimed to have been lurking about my letter box coming unbidden to my mind.

He looked like a foreigner of some kind to me, with his tanned skin and black eyes, the old woman had said of that mysterious stranger. *His hair was black, too; as black as the Devil's own.*

"Until I found them in a San Francisco antique shop," I finished lamely, the falsehood sounding forced and unreal even to my own ears. "Why? Are they a find of some sort? A long-lost strand of Greek kombo-loi worth a fortune?" I tried to make my voice light but I couldn't, the strain I felt at having him here like this in my room, his face dark and stormy and accusing, causing me to be more wary of him than ever.

It was as though he imagined me to be a thief in addition to being a fortune hunter who had come here hoping to claim some part of my dead grandfather's estate.

His next words seemed only to confirm my thumbnail analysis of the thoughts I pictured running through his mind. "I think you know as well as I do that this is no ordinary string of worry beads." He waved the strand of amber accusingly in my face.

"If you're assuming that I know antiques, I don't," I stated flatly.

"You can't be that ignorant of the Blackhurst heirlooms," he said, his mouth crooking into a cynical little smile. "Surely you are aware that you've succeeded in unearthing the Blackhurst Ambers, whatever else you may have expected to find with all of your stealthy rummaging."

Before I could move away from him, he flung the glowing beads around my neck and used them to try to pull me to him.

I yielded when I felt the string that held them begin to give. But if I had expected him to kiss me again, some hidden, eager part of me wanting that against my conscious will, I was disappointed.

Instead, he stared deeply into my face, as though it was his intention to lay bare any secrets I might have.

"I suggest you put these in a safe place," he finally said, releasing me so abruptly that I had to step swiftly backward to keep my balance.

Turning abruptly toward the door, he left me, going with quick, long strides into the hallway, closing the heavy panels softly behind him.

Numbly I realized that he had forgotten to tell me why he had wanted to see me. In any case, it no longer seemed to matter.

My only thought now was that someone in this house had gone to San Francisco with the intention of intercepting my mother's letters, just as Mrs. Costain had suspected. More shattering still, that same person had tried to kill me. The beads that I had found knotted into a hangman's noose around my neck when Guy Lannin arrived to rescue me had told me that; the same beads that Gabe Guirlande had slipped over my head this evening and that still slithered coldly against my flesh. Suddenly they seemed to contain some malevolent power of their own to destroy me.

Tearing the Blackhurst Ambers from around my neck, I thrust them into one of the empty candy boxes and closed the lid on them, as though they were a poisonous snake coiled to strike.

Chapter ELEVEN

Seena was alone at breakfast when I went down the following morning. It had been a disturbed night; I had been besieged by a barrage of nightmarish thoughts and speculations, all of them revolving around my missing mother and the veiled threats which had been made against me.

"It appears that I shall have you all to myself this morning, Tracey," my aunt said amiably when I took my place beside her. "Gabe has ridden into the fields to check on the hands, and the others haven't yet risen." She reached to fill one of the fragile Sevres cups with Odalie's fragrant coffee. "There's chicory in it," she said of the thick black brew. "Gabe likes to refer to it as *fort comme la mort.*"

Strong as death.

I said quickly, "Gabe is staying here at Blackhurst Hall, then."

"He thought it might be a good idea to move in here for awhile," Seena said. "Especially since there are so many odds and ends to attend to now that your grandfather is gone. Death is such a complicated business for those of us who remain behind." She gave a weary little sigh. "But let's speak of more pleasant things. Tell me, Tracey. How is Lorainne? What does she do with herself, now that she's a widow as I am? I've been wanting this opportunity to ask you about her. It's been so long since we last saw each other."

"I'd really rather not talk about her right now, if you don't mind," I said. "After all, she is missing. And I can't help but be concerned about her," I added, unable to keep a note of rebuke from shading my voice.

"But we all are." Seena's carefully plucked brows tightened into an expression of distress. "I for one am more worried than you know. Such dreadful things happen to people these days. Did you call San Francisco, as I suggested?"

"Twice," I said, having tried calling home again the previous evening.

"You've arranged to have any mail you might receive from her forwarded to you here, I presume," Seena said.

I nodded. "This really isn't at all like her, you know. And the fact that the two letters I had from her before I left were postmarked St. Bridges makes her disappearance seem all the more inexplicable."

"You must know that she had friends here in St. Bridges before she met and married your father," Seena said, her manner seeming slightly abstracted.

"Perhaps you could give me the names of some of them," I said eagerly. "Anyone who may have been especially close to her."

"I'm afraid I can't be of much help to you, darling," Seena said. "Lorainne was so much younger than I that I really didn't get to know any of her friends that well, although I vaguely recall seeing them around." She shrugged helplessly. "I really am sorry about all of this, Tracey. But I'm sure you'll come up with something that will lead you to her."

"You still think she's gone off somewhere with a man, don't you?" I said, a trifle bitterly.

"What would you expect me to think under the circumstances?" Seena countered. "You're still very young, perhaps too young to realize that people don't always behave in a way which we sometimes like to think of as 'in character.'"

I saw that there was no point in arguing with her. Her mind was made up about my mother, and there was nothing that I could say to her to change it.

I said, after a brief silence during which Odalie appeared with bacon and eggs which we both ignored, "Magda told me about her engagement to Gabe yesterday. I suppose the two of them will be getting married soon, now that he's needed here to help with the running of the plantation." I gestured vaguely in the direction of the billowing canefields, where machines could be heard revving noisily in the distance.

"Magda told you that?" Seena raised her brows at me.

I nodded. "She seemed to think it was something I should know."

"They haven't formally announced their engagement, although I'm certain the two of them have made some plans I don't yet know about," Seena said obscurely.

Reaching for a piece of toast, I broke off a corner and put it absently into my mouth, thinking that there were too many uncertainties in this house. Why should Magda have told me she was engaged to Gabriel Guirlande when her own mother was not yet aware of their plans? Was it because my older cousin saw me as a threat to her desire to claim Gabe for herself? But that was preposterous.

And there were too many unanswered questions in this house too, I thought. One of them concerned my fourth cousin, whom I had yet to meet. So far, none of them had so much as mentioned that cousin's name to me. It was as though all of those who lived in Blackhurst Hall were involved in some finespun conspiracy to withhold any information from me which might help me to know them better. Even my mother, when she had returned home from Blackhurst Hall following my grand-mother's funeral, had seemed reluctant to answer my questions about Seena and my cousins. It was then that I had first noticed a hesitancy in her whenever I asked her to tell me about the house and her life here as a child. Always before she had been straightforward in her answers.

Now I found myself wondering if it were possible that Seena and my cousins had taken it into their heads that I might want to remain here indefinitely, should they give me the least encouragement. I was, after all, as much a Blackhurst as any one of them. Yet why should they fear me so?

Unable to contain my curiosity, I said now to Seena, "I suppose my fourth cousin is off somewhere at school, since the two of us haven't yet met."

Seena's face paled to a chalky whiteness.

160

For a startled moment or two, I thought she would faint.

"What is it?" I asked anxiously.

"Rhea," she said, in a small, gasping voice. "I'm not accustomed to having people remind me . . ." She focused her pale stare on my face, her look a queer mixture of pain and apprehension. "Lorainne didn't tell you then?" she asked. For a moment I could only watch her, aware that I had bungled awkwardly into an area which her manner told me was forbidden to any but the most ignorant and brash.

"Nothing," I said cautiously.

"It was an accident. A *terrible* accident," Seena added in a small, quavering voice.

I wanted to question her further about the accident which had evidently taken the life of my cousin Rhea. But I feared that my aunt might lose control completely were I to pursue it.

Instead I said, "I'm certain my mother didn't know. Otherwise she'd have told me."

Oddly enough, my words appeared to reassure Seena, for she was able then to say in a voice which had gained in strength, "It happened some time ago, even before your grandmother died."

My mother had known then, I thought. She could not have helped but know, since she had come back here to Blackhurst Hall shortly after my grandmother's death. Yet upon her return to San Francisco she had not told either my father or me that one of my cousins had been killed in an accident. I could not help wondering then what manner of accident it had been. Had my cousin died horribly, so horribly that neither Seena nor my mother could bring themselves to relate the details? It had to have been something like that, of course. I could not help being curious in a slightly morbid way about both my cousin and the accident which had caused her to die, perhaps because I sensed that it had affected them all in a way that I could not fully comprehend knowing only the sparse details Seena had provided.

Nevertheless, in the light of what Seena had just told me and as unsatisfactory as those few poignant remarks had been, I found myself viewing both my aunt and my cousins with a greater sympathy than I had been able to feel for them before. I had been right about this house. Death and tragedy were no strangers here. The thought filled me with gloom, and quickly finishing my coffee, I rose to go, leaving

Seena so deeply absorbed in her own depressing thoughts that I doubted if she was even aware that I had gone.

I decided after I had bathed to drive into St. Bridges to find out if anyone there remembered having seen my mother the night she had called to tell me she was waiting at the bus station for one of my cousins to drive her to Blackhurst Hall. Putting on white sandals and a voile, wraparound dress with butterfly sleeves and a high waistline, I started down the stairs on my way to ask Seena for the loan of a car.

I was halfway down the magnificently curving flight when Valmir appeared above me. "Good morning, Tracey," he called to me across the polished banister. "Where are you off to at this ungodly hour?"

"It's nearly ten," I said.

"You haven't answered my question," he said. Although there was nothing in either his face or his voice to suggest that he might be checking on me, I had the feeling as I had had yesterday when Magda had followed me into the gardens, that all of them were watching me. Including Gabe. Why else should he have knocked on my door late last night, unless he had wanted to make certain that I was there where I belonged, in my room sleeping?

I said, "I thought I'd drive into town if I can borrow a car from someone."

"No problem." He started down the stairs toward me. "I'll drive you there myself."

"No," I said too sharply. "You must have things of your own you want to do," I added then, glancing at his expensive knit slacks which were a soft, ivory color.

He wore a brown silk shirt with square ivory buttons and contrast top-stitching. The effect was of wealthy indolence, as though, I thought facetiously, he had nothing better to do with himself than to sit in the cool of the veranda and sip mint juleps all day.

"Have you something special planned?" he asked curiously, his gaze going over me. "You look especially delicious," he added in his practiced way.

"A little personal shopping is all," I said, hoping that would discourage him, even as I found myself responding to his flirtatious charm in a way that I had not intended, my hand rising, seemingly of its own accord, to arrange the thick mass of black hair which hung over my shoulders. "I'm sure it would only bore you."

The truth was that I wanted to carry out the errand I had set for myself in private, apart from those who lived in this house. If it should happen that one of them were responsible in some way for my mother's unexplained disappearance, I did not want that person to know what I was about in my attempts to find her.

"There are other things I could do while I waited," Valmir persisted.

"Another time, perhaps." I smiled brightly at him. "I think I'd like that. Having you show me St. Bridges. I'm certain there must be interesting things there to see, aside from the usual statue in the courthouse square."

He watched me closely for a moment or two. "You can level with me, Tracey," he finally said.

"I don't know what you mean," I said quickly.

"If it's your intention to speak to Gabe concerning *Grandpère*'s estate, I can tell you now, it will get you nowhere," he said.

"Nothing like that had occurred to me," I said truthfully. "In any case, Gabe isn't at his office. Seena told me he's gone into the fields."

"Don't be taken in by his feverish dedication to duty," Valmir said pleasantly enough. "I'm beginning to suspect he has something else in mind, other than giving us a neighborly hand in our hour of grief."

"Like marrying Magda, perhaps," I said without thinking.

"If it would help him to get what he wants," Valmir said.

"And what is that?" I asked.

"Why don't you ask Gabe?" he countered. Almost at once, his charming smile slid into place, the hardness that had masked his features for the barest instant dissolving in a flash of his white teeth. "But then, what Gabe wants isn't really that important, is it? I much prefer discussing you, Tracey. What is it *you* want, *couzan?* As I told you before, I'm at your disposal. You need only to tell me what it is."

"Is that a proposition, Valmir?" a threatening voice said.

I looked up past the twining risers to see Valerie watching us from behind the precariously poised elevator, her features scored by the intricate, lacy pattern of the iron grille. I wondered how long she had been there, spying down on us with a look that was frankly venomous.

"You must forgive Valerie," Valmir said. "She's never at her best this early in the day."

"While Valmir is always at his best, when

it comes to misleading gullible females," Valerie retorted, starting toward us down the stair.

She wore cream and brown as Valmir did, their outfits identical as they had been the first time I saw them together. I wondered whose idea it was for them to dress alike, Valmir's or Valerie's? On Valerie, the colors were less becoming, perhaps because of the emotions I saw smoldering behind her small, pointed features, emotions that seemed in some indefinable way to make her look pinched and drawn.

Almost as though it were his deliberate intention to torment her, Valmir laid his arm lightly across my shoulders. "Come along, Tracey. You can take my car this morning. I'll take you to it."

The car Valmir showed me stood in the old coach house, which had been converted to serve as a garage. Next to it was a sleek black Jaguar which I guessed belonged to Magda even before Valmir told me it was hers.

I wanted to ask him, as I slid behind the wheel of the vintage Thunderbird he said was his, whether it belonged to Valerie as well, not certain that I should accept his offer should it happen that the car belonged to both.

I had not come here to make enemies, only to find my mother. In any case, I could not do that without a car to drive, I rationalized, taking the key he handed me and slipping it into the ignition.

He waved to me as I drove off, his dark and aristocratic features reminding me in some odd way of the face of a Napoleonic soldier in a Géricault painting. I returned his salute, surprised to realize that I was drawn to him in a way I had not expected to be. I glimpsed in him something of the romantic, with his vague dreams of revival in the midst of reconstruction. If it were left to Valmir, I thought, no time would be wasted in returning the old plantation to some semblance of its former glory — if the family coffers could withstand the drain.

Beyond that, I did not doubt for a single moment that Valmir would prove to be delightful company, had I the inclination and the time to spend with him. His easy smile and flirtatious manner told me that much, serving as a pleasant counterpoint that offset Valerie's smoldering fierceness and those half-hidden savage instincts that I had glimpsed in both Magda and Gabe Guirlande.

The drive to St. Bridges proved to be far

168

more pleasant than I had anticipated, considering the nature of my mission. In my haste to reach my sick mother's bedside, during the taxi ride which had brought me here, I had taken little notice of the haunting bayou country.

Now as I steered the powerful Thunderbird along the curving bayou banks, passing an occasional Cajun farmhouse with the inevitable deep *galerie* running the whole width across its front, I became more acutely aware than ever of Blackhurst Hall's lonely isolation in the midst of the sultry cypress swamps. My mother had told me very little about the people who lived here, although she had provided me with odd and intriguing bits of lore from time to time, when I had questioned her about her childhood. I knew for instance that the swamps were haunted by *feux follets* and *loups-garous*, and that the Spanish moss draped from the gnarled limbs of the live oaks and cypress trees had come from the tresses of a lovelorn Indian maiden. Even though I believed neither in luminous spirits nor werewolves, I found the ancient tales fascinating, and as I steered the car on the high ground which wound through the marshlands, the atmosphere was made eerie because of them.

I had almost succeeded in frightening myself, so that I experienced a distinct sense of relief when the road soared again onto the *banquette* which traced the path of a lazy, green bayou through billowing acres of sugar cane. The mushrooming tanks of an oil refinery appeared in the distance, marking the site of the small town, the ultramodern plant incongruous when contrasted with the printed funeral notice I saw tacked onto a lamp post, an ancient custom that I had thought no longer existed.

I had brought a fairly recent photograph of my mother with me in my wallet, and my first stop, when I arrived in St. Bridges, was at the small café at the edge of town, in front of which dangled a sign saying "Bus Depot."

"Her bus must have left her off after we closed that night," the girl behind the counter said, shaking her head slowly from side to side as she stared at my mother's picture. "We don't get that many passengers here, especially at night. This whole place goes to bed with the chickens, except for a few long-haired kids who hang out at a dance hall they've fixed up on the other end of town. And like I say, the bus lets what few there are off out there in front

170

when the place is closed." She gestured in the direction of the street where a telephone booth was visible beside the street lamp on the opposite corner.

"Thank you anyway," I said, unable to conceal my disappointment.

"Look, I'm sorry I couldn't be of more help, really I am," the girl said, staring out through the windows. "Hey, isn't that Valmir Verret's car you're driving?" she added, giving me a curious look.

"I borrowed it for the day," I said.

"What did that sister of his have to say about that?" Her voice rose on a note of vicarious triumph. "That Valmir is something else, isn't he? But that Valerie . . ." She broke off, her eyes rolling toward the ceiling. "She's always right there waiting to pounce on any girl who dares to show any interest in him."

"The Verrets are my cousins," I said coolly, primly refusing to be drawn into her gossip.

"Listen, I didn't mean anything by what I said," the girl called after me when I turned to go.

I glanced at her across my shoulder. "I'm sure you didn't," I said shortly, noticing how red her face had become above her faded green uniform, whose seams appeared to be on the verge of splitting, strained in an effort to contain her over-weight body.

"You all hurry back now, d'ya hear," she went on condescendingly.

This time I did not bother to reply, thinking that it was scarcely likely that Valmir was apt to pay any attention to her, regardless of what she dared to do.

Methodically then, I drove down the town's main street, stopping at each place of business, taking my wallet from my purse and holding out the photograph of my mother for the store-owners to study.

But it was the same wherever I went. No one could recall having seen my mother, although one or two of the older mer-chants remembered who she was when I told them her name.

It had been late evening in San Fran-cisco when she had called me from here on the night of her arrival. Making allowances for the time difference, I estimated that she must have arrived in St. Bridges shortly after midnight. Because she had not both-ered to let Seena know ahead of time that she was coming, she had no doubt called Blackhurst Hall from the airport upon her arrival in New Orleans to ask someone there to meet her bus. One of my cousins was coming for her, she had told me on the telephone. But which one of them was it? Or had Gabe Guirlande been there that night? Was he the one who had taken her call, pretending to be Valmir when my mother had told him who she was and what she wanted? If so, why? What treacherous game was he playing?

I sat behind the wheel of the Thunderbird trying to decide where to turn next. I had already called the hospital, only to discover that no one there had ever heard of her. Now it seemed that I had reached a dead end.

Briefly I considered going to the police. Then I decided against it, when it occurred to me that my mother might have her own reasons for remaining hidden from me, reasons that could prove to be embarrassing to her should they somehow serve to confirm Seena's worst suspicions about her. It was for that reason alone that I refrained from driving to the local police station to tell them how frightened I was.

I would give myself another day or two to try to locate her, I decided. Then if I still had not succeeded in finding her, or at least a clue which might serve to tell me where she had gone, I would consider going to the police with my story.

Meanwhile, there seemed to be nothing left for me to do but to return to Blackhurst Hall, whose dark aura threatened to swallow me.

Chapter TWELVE

The house was quiet when I returned shortly after one, having bought myself a hamburger for lunch at a roadside stand.

"Miss Seena say to tell you she's got one of her headaches should you ask for her," Odalie, busy in the hallway with her dust cloths and vacuum, told me when I entered through the front door. "Don't do no good to ask me where the others gone to. Miss Seena and Miss Magda had one of their quarrels, and everybody scatter like chickens in a rainstorm when Miss Magda got one of her mads on. Most likely though, Mr. Valmir and Miss Valerie gone off again to look for Lafitte's gold in the middle of the swamps, and I heard Miss Magda ride off on her horse a short while ago."

"What about Mr. Guirlande?" I asked. "Is he with my aunt?"

"Mr. Gabe left for his office awhile back," Odalie said. "Ain't nobody with Miss Seena. That's the way she want it when she takes one of her headache pills.

They're powerful strong, them," she added, slipping unconsciously into the local Cajun idiom.

I thought that if my dead cousin Rhea had left her mark on this house, so had her father, Ves Verret.

I said, "I'm not used to this sticky heat. Perhaps I'll lie down for awhile myself."

"Won't anybody disturb you," Odalie said. "Miss Seena likes the house quiet when she's indisposed."

The house seemed almost eerily silent as I went up the stairs. In the back of my mind was the thought that with my cousins and Gabe Guirlande out of the house and Seena lying down in her room, there was nothing to stop me from making a surreptitious search of Blackhurst Hall's upper stories.

I did not hesitate. I suppose the thought was in my mind that if I stopped to consider what I intended to do, I might lose my courage, which was none too hardy to begin with. Going quickly along the second-floor passage, I turned to the left a short distance past my door, into the corridor which connected the west wing with the main part of the house. I was still haunted by the pale form I had seen lurking behind the dark vines which sheltered the west wing gallery, Nor could I so easily forget the whispering voice I had heard coming to me from behind the west wing's locked windows, a voice which belonged to someone who claimed her name was Amber.

Islands of chairs and small tables appeared in the dim shadows before me, and there was a Louis XVI sofa, its padded seat and back covered with faded needlepoint, standing beside a tall, cartouched clock fitted with brass ornaments.

Farther ahead of me, their heavily framed panels shaped to fit the arch of the ceiling, were the matching double doors which I knew would take me into the west wing. I think I knew even before I reached to pry at their scrolled silver handles, that I would find them locked securely against me. Pitting all of my strength against their ancient hardware, I tried to force the doors apart.

But it was no use. The bolt securing them refused stubbornly to release.

I paused to listen then, pressing my ear against the seam between the twin panels. A tense silence seemed to hover around me, broken only by the violent thudding of my own heart.

Was it possible that someone lived alone in the mansion's sealed west wing? And if

177

so, could it conceivably be that it was my mother who had hidden herself away there? Had the illness she had mentioned to me in her letter been of the mind rather than of the body, as I had assumed it was at the time? It was possible, I supposed, that my grandfather's death might have proved to be too much for her. Yet how could she do this to me? Unless her condition had worsened to a point where she no longer remembered that she had a daughter, or even what her own rightful name was, I thought chillingly.

As preposterous as that particular possibility seemed, I was unwilling to discredit even the slimmest ray of hope that I might find her hidden away somewhere inside this monstrous old house, and I stayed where I was, my ears strained to catch even the least hint of a sound which might tell me she was there.

I imagined then that I heard a slight movement somewhere behind the thick panels, and, although I could not be certain that it had been anything more than a figment of my imagination generated by my feverish determination to find out where she had gone, I called softly.

Nothing.

I called again, "Mother, it's Tracey.

Please, whoever you are, answer me."

Again, nothing, apart from the uneasy silence which had grown heavy with the heated scents from the garden so that it had become virulent, as though it were weighted with some secret life of its own.

Feeling uncomfortable, I turned away, unable to put aside the feeling that someone lurked on the far side of the heavy doors, someone who did not want to answer me.

Trying desperately to recall everything my mother had ever told me about the house, I remembered that there was a servants' stairway from the butler's pantry behind the kitchen that led upward between the thick, brick walls to the west wing's second story.

Moving as quietly as I could, I hurried back down the stairs. The hum of Odalie's vacuum came to me now from the front parlor. Grateful for the spaciousness of the house which permitted me to slip unnoticed into the murky shadows behind the elevator well, I went swiftly through the dining room into the narrow back passageway off which both the kitchen and pantry doors opened.

But it was not to be that easy. The door which opened off the butler's pantry to provide access to the steeply winding servants' stairway was securely locked against me.

The only alternative left to me if I were to gain access to the west wing was through the tall French windows which opened off the second-floor gallery. Already I knew that it would be pointless for me to try to gain access there. For reasons that I could only try to guess, the west wing was tightly sealed, as though to provide an impenetrable bastion for whoever might be hiding there inside its darkly shrouded walls.

Turning away from the locked door at the foot of the back stair, my thoughts went next to the attic. With Seena incapacitated in her room and the others still absent from the house, it seemed an ideal time for me to search for some clue my mother might have left for me to find, should whoever had met her bus that night have brought her here without the others' knowledge.

The main staircase continued upward to the mansion's third story, curving sinuously around the deep, central well where the elevator hung suspended from its frayed ropes and ornate pulleys.

Arriving slightly out of breath, I paused

on the third-floor landing in an attempt to gain my bearings. A series of family portraits hung against the creamy, plastered walls of the spacious foyer. I gazed curiously into the faces of my Blackhurst ancestors, finding no hint of Cajun blood here. Several of the subjects had coloring similar to my own, their prim, Scots faces framed bounteously with black hair which served to emphasize the misty paleness of their skin.

I guessed that the deceased family members I gazed upon now were among the lesser known Blackhursts, possibly even black sheep, their likenesses relegated here perhaps by Seena, in conjunction with her efforts to modernize the tyrannical old monstrosity, as my mother had called the house.

One of the plantation gentlemen held a dusty cotton boll in his hand, while yet another of the handsome Blackhurst men, his face expressionless above his black stock, leaned rakishly on a gold-knobbed cane, something in his manner reminding me of Valmir.

Pulling myself away from the paintings, I went toward wide double doors which stood slightly ajar as though someone had recently had reason to come here. Pushing them cautiously inward, I peered between them into the dusky dimness of what had once been a ballroom of enormous proportions, its ceiling and walls plastered to follow the sloping contours of the house's mansard roofline.

Deeply arched openings at regular intervals along the ballroom's side walls provided access to jutting dormer windows so heavily swathed in straggling cobwebs and folds of fraying brocade that their narrow alcoves yawned like vaulted caverns.

I touched a switch beside the door. A single bulb flashed on in the huge crystal chandelier which dominated the center of the slanting ceiling, its glow diminished to a grayish pall by the intricate arrangement of cobwebs clinging to the dangling prisms. My first impression was of having stepped backward into a world gone topsy-turvy, its disorder softened by time into a dim reality, like the pale figures which decorated the handpainted wallpaper panels beside the stair's winding risers.

Remnants of the magnificent life my ancestors had once enjoyed in this house were all around me, manifested in a vast array of trunks and boxes and broken furniture. I glimpsed ponderous pieces of carved mahogany, upholstered in horsehair so badly demolished by mice that only a few frayed strands of the wiry stuffing were left clinging to the ornate frames.

Odd pieces of broken statuary loomed out of the dark tangle like pale ghosts rising from some dismal carnage, and there was a monstrous mirror set in a filigree frame, its glass cracked into a pattern that resembled a huge, dark bird in flight. Reminded against my will of the ominous black bird that had lighted on my windowsill the day I received that last puzzling letter from my mother, I turned sharply away from my own distorted image, overwhelmed just as I had been then by a sudden sense of evil.

But I would not give in to those treacherous thoughts. Not now, when I needed all of the courage I could possibly muster if I were to continue with my search here in the midst of these depressing relics.

The attic is chock full of mementoes, my mother had said of this huge, cluttered room. *Old songbooks filled with sentimental ballads and ancient prayer books spilling out dusty clusters of forget-me-nots and gardenias . . . even a few frayed remnants of the first bride's trousseau.*

Amber, my mother had told me when I had asked her that first bride's name.

Amber, the eerily whispering voice had said to me from behind the west wing windows.

Was it coincidental that the man who had tried to strangle me before I left San Francisco had chosen as his weapon a necklace made of amber? A necklace which, according to Gabe Guirlande, was a Blackhurst family heirloom? What did it mean? That one of them, perhaps even Gabe himself, had come to San Francisco determined not only to intercept my mother's letters before they could reach me, but to be rid of me as well?

As well . . . Icy fingers seemed suddenly to touch me, and for the first time I admitted to myself that it was possible that my mother was not only missing, but dead.

Frantically, without knowing what it was I sought, I began to search, driven by a nameless dread which had somehow wormed its way into my conscious thoughts.

A carved sandalwood chest set deep inside one of the dormer alcoves caught my eye, perhaps because it looked as though it might once have served to hold a bride's trousseau. Going quickly to open it, I was disappointed to find nothing more than a few broken fans and an assortment of old greeting cards and lace-paper valentines.

Moving deeper into the shadowy alcove, I came onto an ancient camelback trunk. Even in that faint light, I could not help noticing that its top had recently been wiped free of dust. A queer, surging sense of excitement took hold of me as I knelt beside it to pry with trembling fingers at its hinged latches. For a shattering moment or two, I imagined, when the central hasp refused to give, that the trunk was locked.

Then, without warning, the tarnished lock sprung free and I was able to lift the cumbersome lid and peer inside.

Disappointingly, the trunk appeared at first glance to contain nothing more than an odd assortment of ancient gowns and toques, the artificial flowers attached to the crushed brims of the elaborate old bonnets faded beyond recognition.

Nevertheless, there was something about the carefully folded garments which caught my attention. I realized then that it was because they appeared to be meticulously cared for, for all of their outmoded style and faded silk blossoms. Surprisingly, someone had cared enough about the old dresses to place layers of yellowed tissue paper along their folds. Furthermore, it quickly became apparent to me when I lifted the top gowns to peer deeper into the trunk, that several of the dresses had never been worn.

An essence of fragrant femininity seemed in some incalculable way to cling to the rustling silks and laces, which smelled faintly of Attar of Roses. Very little light penetrated the alcove, and I went impatiently to draw aside the dust-encrusted draperies at its far end, tucking the thick brocade, streaked with mildew where it had lain against the grimy windowpanes into a corner of the wide frame.

Rays of greenish gray light found their way uncertainly through the time-misted glass that had not been washed in so long that it had become very nearly opaque. Although I wished for a stronger light by which to examine the trunk's contents, this would have to do, and I went quickly to kneel again on the dusty floorboards, my exploring fingers unearthing an old songbook tacked beneath a tissue-wrapped bouquet.

There was not the least doubt in my mind then that I had succeeded in uncovering the mementoes my mother had once told me about, and which she had wanted to believe had belonged to that first bride whose name was Amber. More shattering still, these were mementoes which someone in this house had had reason to examine recently, I thought. The absence of dust on the trunk's humped lid had told me that. Had that someone been my mother? In which case, had one of my cousins appeared in St. Bridges the night of her arrival to bring her back here, after all, in spite of what Gabe and Seena had wanted me to believe? Was this old trunk with its carefully preserved reminders of that first bride the clue I sought to confirm what she had told me in her letters; that she was here in this house somewhere even now, patiently awaiting my arrival in her worst hour of need?

The thoughts rioting through my mind filled me with a queer, cold sense of desperation. Laying aside the cluster of dried flowers which were still recognizable as the forget-me-nots and gardenias my mother had mentioned to me, I reached again for the old songbook. Opening its cover gently because of its great age, I searched for an inscription which would tell me to whom it had once belonged.

The script that I had hoped to find was there, flowing in an intricate pattern of scrolls and swirls across the top of the title page. Unable to decipher the faded handwriting in that eerie wash of greenish light,

I went with it to the window, rubbing my palm against one of the scabrous panes to clear away the scum.

To Ambre, my angel, my dove, the elaborately flowing script said. *Your faithful guardian, Charles Beecher Blackhurst.*

Ambre. I recognized the French for Amber. My excitement rising, I leafed through the book's fragile pages, which consisted of a number of yellowing sheets of music that had been bound together, their individual title pages decorated lavishly with twining garlands of roses and gamboling cupids.

Briefly I scanned stanzas devoted to moonlight and nightingales and love unrequited, aware of a certain aura of sadness engendered by the sentimental ballads. *Les Belles de la Côte Joyeuse,* read a title facing a section of the book which was devoted to a series of waltzes dedicated to a girl with the unlikely name of Nazilda.

Putting the songbook aside for the moment, I delved deeper into the old trunk, taking care not to disturb the carefully folded gowns lying on top. A thrill of anticipation went through me when my probing fingers encountered a small, velour-bound volume tucked into the bottom of the trunk, as though whoever had been here recently to dust off its top had wanted to hide it from someone. I could not imagine anyone in this house being especially interested in the trunk's contents. Certainly not Seena, with her admitted passion for things modern. Nor did it seem likely that any one of my cousins might have fallen prey to a nostalgia which might have brought him or her here to browse through the attic's jumbled relics. My mother was the only person I could think of who might have had reason recently to examine the contents of Amber's trunk, if only because they represented a part of her childhood which she had once related to me.

I wondered, as I withdrew the diary with fingers that had begun suddenly to tremble, if it was at all possible that my mother might have left some special message for me here, during the time since I had last seen her. Or was I allowing my imagination to run away with me, in my desperation to find out where she had gone?

It seemed then that I could not open the diary quickly enough, so intense was my desire to discover some hidden message from her, and I pried at its fragile hasp with fingers that not only trembled, but that had become inordinately clumsy. It was a moment or two before I could succeed in prying apart the fragile pages.

Ambre Aurore Lestant. The name scrawled across the flower-embellished flyleaf was written in a bold, feminine hand. Although my knowledge of French was minimal, I associated the name with Creoles who had settled this part of the state.

Quickly I sifted through the diary's pages. But if I had expected to find a folded sheet of my mother's blue monogrammed stationery tucked inside, I was disappointed. There was no hidden message for me, apart from the confidences set down on the gold-leafed pages by that long-ago girl named Amber, a girl someone in this house wanted me to believe still lived. I could not help recalling the pale form I had seen on the west wing gallery, who had claimed in a queerly whispering voice to be Amber.

This is to be a chronicle of my new life, the diary began. *Nous sommes maintenant en janvier. Le premier mois de l'année . . .*

We are now in January, I translated. *The first month of the year . . .*

Much to my relief, the diary continued in English. My impression then was of a girl who had sought to rearrange her life in accordance with her new circumstances by dropping a language with which she had long been familiar in favor of English.

I, Ambre Aurore Lestant, age sixteen, have come on this 11th day of January to live at Blackhurst Hall as Charles Blackhurst's ward, the next sentence read.

Slightly stunned when it suddenly occurred to me for the first time that Blackhurst Hall's first bride had not been a Blackhurst at all, but a *ward,* I scanned quickly ahead. *The house seemed vast and empty when I arrived, but with Charles here to greet me, I could not be sad and lonely for long,* Amber had written in her boldly feminine hand.

Charles. Not Mr. Blackhurst, nor even Papa, as I should have imagined a sixteen-year-old ward might have referred to the man who had, as the diary seemed to imply, only recently been appointed her guardian. There was something in the very way Amber had penned his name that alerted me, and it occurred to me how little my mother had actually told me about her.

Charles insisted that the two of us indulge in a little champagne, Amber's diary continued. *As everyone knows, champagne is the most treacherous of all wines, a fact which was soon made plain to me by the sudden change*

191

in Charles' attitude. He had made love to me before, but not like this.

I paused. My mother had read these lines before me, I thought. She had known that my ancestor, the man who had founded Blackhurst Plantation and built the house, had fallen in love with a sixteen-year-old girl who had been his ward. I wondered if she had been scandalized, as I was, not because I was puritanical in my own moral outlook. But because it had never occurred to me that one of my stoic Blackhurst ancestors might ever have become romantically involved outside the sacred bonds of matrimony, least of all with a sixteen-year-old girl for whom he had been appointed guardian.

It was exactly the kind of tale that belonged between the pages of a Southern novel, I thought facetiously, as I continued to read.

Charles is enchanted with me, Amber had set down in her confidently scrawling hand. A picture of her was already forming in my mind, not as the frail, virginal bride I had always imagined her to be, but as a spirited young girl who had had very definite ideas about what she wanted from life. And had fully expected to receive, I could not help thinking as my gaze continued to follow the unwavering trails of faded script.

Charles refers to me always as his little dove, his angel, his love, Amber had written. *He is so deeply enchanted with me that he has promised one day soon to marry me. I shall be mistress of this grand house then, and those hateful daughters of his shan't dare ever to slight me again. Charles knows how deeply I am resented by them and shall do everything in his power to see that they grant me the respect deserved by a good wife.*

There was something almost childish and naive in what Amber had written. At the same time I was aware of a willful determination, guessing that she must have been beautiful and had known how to use her looks to turn Charles Blackhurst's head.

It is unthinkable even to imagine that I shall be a stepmother to Charles' children, the diary said next. *Particularly since they are all of them older than my own parents should have been had they survived the cholera as I did. I am certain that none of them shall ever feel inclined to call me maman!*

I have seen how envious and jealous Charles' eldest daughter is of me, another entry said. *As if it were in some way my own doing that I was born beautiful. Can I help it if my hair is the color of clover honey and my complexion flawless? If the rest of them hate me, Charles makes up for their lack of breeding by lavishing me with praises. He is charmingly mannered and an altogether pleasant man, for all of his great age. I shan't mind too much having a husband who is old enough to be my grandfather, particularly since he showers me with jewelry to show his appreciation of my comeliness and youth. His latest gift is a necklace of amber. The beads are the same shade as my hair, although they seem frightfully wicked, filled as they are with vicious-looking little insects that appear as though they are preparing to sting somebody.*

The beads belong to me, the voice that had whispered to me from behind the west wing windows had told me. Amber's voice, whispering to me from out of the past?

But that was impossible. I did not believe in ghosts, nor was I prepared to start believing in them now.

Then who was it who had fled from me along the west wing gallery, to vanish behind the tall French windows before I could guess his or her identity?

Partly because there was not enough time for me to read the diary in its entirety, partly because the entries became even more personal in an impishly narcissistic

194

way which portrayed Amber not at all as I had first imagined her, but as a slightly wicked child-woman who was willing to marry her elderly guardian for the position she had coveted, I closed the covers on the brittle pages.

Taking care to replace the diary in the trunk exactly as I had found it, I laid the songbook on top of it and arranged the folded garments to cover both. The contents of the diary had emphasized to me the exquisite richness of the rustling silks and laces that I knew now had belonged to Amber, gifts for her trousseau, no doubt, from my besotted ancestor, as were the amber beads which someone had used in an attempt to strangle me.

One of the gowns was of amber satin, with double flounces of sheer black lace falling to form a bertha collar below scandalously low-cut shoulders. A huge silk rose, its gauze petals and leaves irretrievably crushed by the weight of the trunk's rounded lid, decorated the gown's tight, boned bodice.

It was far too easy for me to picture the girl who had worn it, her flawless features framed with saucy, honey-toned ringlets.

Closing the trunk on those piteous remnants of a life that I sensed had somehow gone awry, I went quickly to replace the dusty drapes over the window.

Taking a last look about to make certain that my tracks were covered, lest whoever had been here before me return to discover that I had been snooping, I went back to the stairs.

Perhaps because I was not accustomed to rummaging about where I had no real business being, a sudden sense of guilt assaulted me as I started downward. It seemed then that I caught the musty scent of faded roses clinging to my skin and clothes. I could not risk having the others guess where I had been, I thought, a slight feeling of panic coming over me.

I had not yet been up to the belvedere where my ancestor had once taken his guests to view the sprawling Blackhurst lands, the treacherous old elevator serving as an innovative means to waft them skyward, and it occurred to me now that the fresh air there might serve to wash away the stale smell of spent lives which seemed to cling stubbornly to me, as though some provocative part of the girl whose diary I had read had risen from out of the depths of the old trunk to haunt me.

Spinning about, I ran swiftly upward, going out through French doors located

196

near the head of the stairs onto the belvedere's ornately balustraded gallery. Gazing out between the swaying fingers of moss hanging from the branches of the ancient live oaks, I breathed deeply of the richly scented air. A movement near the old sugar house distracted me away from the subtle scents which still seemed to cling to my skin and hair. Valmir and Valerie, I thought, catching a glimpse of their matching outfits as they came toward me along a narrow road which penetrated between the cane fields.

Then as quickly as they had appeared, they vanished into the bleak shadows behind the old sugar house, going in the direction of the ancient Indian shell mound where the Blackhurst tombs were located.

Had they decided, upon their return from the swamps, to pay a visit to my grandfather's tomb — or perhaps to lay fresh flowers on their sister Rhea's grave? I wondered vaguely about that, my thoughts going again to that first bride, who, according to my mother, had been laid to rest inside the old family crypt.

Try as I might, I could not pull myself free from the haunting sensation that, regardless of where her remains were buried, Ambre Aurore Lestant still lived in this house.

Chapter THIRTEEN

I woke that same night out of an uneasy sleep, not certain at first what it was that had disturbed me.

I lay stiffly in the big bed, my heart pounding, as an eerie light invaded my room, flickering faintly over the walls beyond the gauzy folds of the mosquito *barre* to cast darkly dancing shadows around me.

For a numbing moment or two, I imagined that yet another of the swiftly gathering thunderstorms had descended on the old house to send angry jags of lightning flashing beyond the thick ranks of greenery.

Then as that first nightmarish sensation passed and I came fully awake, I saw her.

She stood in the open doorway. The filtered light casting dark patterns on the papered walls was coming from the lighted candle she held stiffly before her in the unconsciously defensive attitude of a sleepwalker.

Because I could not see her face clearly in that uncertain light, I imagined at first

198

that it was Seena who stood in my doorway, and my first thought then was that she had come to tell me that the electricity had gone out again.

Then I saw, with a wild wave of disbelief, that she wore the same amber satin gown I had seen earlier, folded carefully into the camelback trunk in the attic. There was no mistaking the filmy folds of the wide bertha collar, which fell away from her alabaster shoulders to etch the pale flesh of her upper arms with a faint, lacy tracery.

Amber! Was I caught up in some incredible dream from which I refused to wake? The disbelief I had felt before was turning swiftly to panic. What was happening to me in this monstrous old house with its seething undercurrents of death and tragedy? What mad tricks were my frightened thoughts playing on me?

Turning my head stealthily sideways in the deep hollow of the goosedown pillow, I looked out between narrowed eyelids in an effort to see more clearly. But if I had expected the ghostly intruder to vanish as mysteriously as she had appeared, to leave my doorway comfortingly empty, I was disappointed.

She remained as she had been when I first became aware of her presence, the candle held before her in that same stiffly cautious way, as though it were her intention to hide behind its leaping shadows. I noticed vaguely that she held the candle with her left hand, keeping her right hand hidden from me behind the billowing folds of her long skirt, and it occurred to me then that she could very well be carrying a weapon which she wished to conceal.

Even though I still could not see her face clearly, lost as it was in the shifting shadows, I knew with certainty that this was no ghostly figment of my imagination but a flesh-and-blood being, palpably real and somehow threatening.

Still caught in the grip of a paralyzing panic, I tried to think what I must do. Who was it from among those who inhabited the old house that wanted to frighten me in this macabre way? Why? Should I speak out boldly to the intruder, demand to know what he or she was doing here?

The thought crossed my mind that I had locked my door before I turned out my lights. Shifting my gaze, I saw the key glittering faintly on the nightstand beside my bed where I had put it before I slid between the sheets. I should have known that there would be other keys in this house which would serve to slip the door's old-fashioned bolt. A simple skeleton key was all that had been required, I thought chillingly.

Nevertheless, I had not expected this ghostly invasion of my privacy, and I thought belatedly how insecure I was in this house, how vulnerable to the mad whims of its occupants. For it seemed plain to me that the person who stood watching me from the doorway, her face hidden from me behind the small, dancing flame which cast it in shadow, was somehow deranged. Why else should whoever it was be wearing the same elaborate gown I had seen earlier in the attic, a gown that had belonged once to Blackhurst's first bride?

I decided then that the safest thing for me to do, at least until I could determine what the invader's intentions toward me were, was to pretend that I still slept. My body tense between the crisp sheets whose faint lavender scent seemed in some peculiar way to increase the cold sense of unreality that enveloped me, I waited, still watching the intruder from between narrowed eyelids.

Slowly she took a step toward me, and another, her right hand still hidden from my view behind the billowing satin. Unconsciously I braced myself, thinking vaguely that whatever her intentions toward me might be, I could not just continue to lie there.

Still I waited, caught in the grip of curiosity. I suppose that somewhere in the back of my mind lurked the thought that the woman who came toward me might yet prove in some inconceivable way to be my mother.

The candle guttered in her outstretched hand, fed by the softly moving air currents raised by her long, rustling skirts. Briefly I glimpsed the pale oval of her face, half-hidden between thick wings of hair that shimmered like molten honey as the firefly glints of light illuminated their silken strands.

Amber! I remembered the description that first bride had given of herself in her diary, a stab of terror going through me, followed by a nightmare wave of unreality.

I wanted to cry out, to demand of her who she was.

But before I could force myself to speak, she said, in that same softly whispering voice I had heard before, coming to me from behind the west wing's locked windows, "Lorainne! You've come back to me."

Lorainne. Numbly I realized that this ghostly intruder imagined me to be my missing mother. What did it mean? That the ghost woman had seen my mother recently, here in this house?

A wild surge of hope swept over me. Throwing caution aside, I sat directly up in bed. Pulling back the mosquito *barre,* I confronted her.

"I'm not Lorainne, I'm Tracey," I said urgently. "Tell me, has Lorainne been here recently? Is that why you imagined I was she?"

For a stunning moment, the ghost woman stayed where she was, staring wildly down at me. In that same paralyzing instant, I glimpsed flawless features devoid of any hint of color, her eyes glittering at me from darkly sunken sockets above cheeks so emaciated that their bones stood out clearly above their deep hollows.

I think I must have cried out then. For abruptly she blew out her candle, plunging the room into a fathomless darkness.

"Tracey?" Her voice whispered chillingly around me. "But I told you to go. Go away! Go away! You can't say I didn't warn you."

Mad! The word echoed soundlessly through my head. *Mad!*

Vaguely I heard the rustle of her skirts as she whirled away from me, followed by the soft whisper of her footsteps as she fled through the open doorway to go scurrying off along the endless hallway.

Collecting my shattered senses, I leapt from the bed to follow, glimpsing her pale form going, not in the direction of the west wing as I had expected her to do, but toward the spiraling staircase which wound upward around the deep, central well of the house.

Pausing only long enough to switch on the light mounted beside my door, I went after her, my bare footsteps falling soundlessly on the Persian runners which formed shadowy, dark pools along the length of the polished floorboards.

I hesitated when I reached the landing, unable now to hear the soft thud of her slippers. Moving silently to the edge of the stairwell where the elevator hung, suspended behind an ornate gate set between the intricately carved balusters, I peered upward, past the darkly curving banister.

But if the ghostly intruder had fled in the direction of the ballroom above, there was no sign of her. Staying where I was, I listened, becoming suddenly aware of a soft, swishing rustle on the risers which wound downward behind me, past the dangling old elevator.

I spun around. But I was too late. In that same paralyzing instant, a dark shape swirled wildly upward above my head and I was enveloped in a smothering blackness which sucked away my breath.

I went down beneath the force of that terrifying onslaught, my head striking against the curlicued metal of the ancient elevator gate with a resounding thud. In the split second before I blacked out, I remembered the tattered black bird that had swooped onto my windowsill in San Francisco, the thought flashing through my head that that dark harbinger of evil had not been sent by Fate to warn me as I had wanted to believe then, but to smother me beneath the spreading black wings of death.

I came to enfolded by darkness. For a pain-dulled moment, I imagined that the sinister dark wings still wrapped themselves around me.

Then, as my senses began slowly to clear, I realized that my face was no longer smothered beneath that terrible, musty furriness and that I was breathing freely.

A soft, creaking sound came to me and I

became aware of a gently swaying motion that seemed somehow ominous. Moving cautiously, partly because the least jarring motion set off rockets of pain flashing behind my temple, partly because I had not the least idea where I was, enveloped as I was by pitch-blackness, I explored my surroundings.

The first thing my icy fingers encountered was the satiny smoothness of slickly varnished wood. A plank, I thought numbly, supported by coiling tendrils of cold metal: The varnished benches inside the old elevator cage where those long-ago ladies and gentlemen had seated themselves while robust slaves rotated the cabledrums at the bottom of the central well in order to waft them skyward.

I sat up cautiously, reaching to explore the area beyond the benches, my fingers finding the ornate, wrought-iron tracings which formed a protective barrier around me.

Now that I had gained my bearings, I was able to distinguish the dark pattern of the winding stair rail etched above and below me against faint patches of graying light which marked the landings of each floor. Working my way cautiously around the sides of the cage, I searched for the grilled gate, my fingers encountering a wadded mass of some softly napped fabric. Velvet, I thought numbly, a musty scent rising around me when I lifted the soft length of cloth.

It became evident to me then that what I had imagined in that shattering, split-second instant before I had lost consciousness to be the furry wings of some hideous dark bird of death had been nothing more than a length of black cloth tossed over my head by my attacker to prevent me from seeing his or her face. I had, in that same split-instant before I blacked out, been aware of a certain strength which had seemed out of keeping with the fragile-appearing ghost woman who had entered my room, imagining me to be my missing mother. Was it possible that the emaciated creature who had stared at me out of sunken eye sockets had put me here? Had the impression I'd had of stick-thin fragility been merely an illusion, created by the faintly flickering candlelight, which had not allowed me to see the intruder clearly?

Whoever my attacker had been, he or she had apparently thrust me into the old elevator and then gone to the house's lower level to set the ancient mechanism into motion to lift me upward, so that I found myself trapped now between the high-ceilinged floors. Even though I might succeed in prying loose the iron bar which secured the grilled gate, there was no possible way that I could leave the elevator, stationed as it was between the stair's wide-spaced landings. It was not a guess, it was a certainty that my attacker's intention had been to trap me. But why? In order to frighten me further so that I would waste no time in packing my bags to leave when I finally succeeded in finding a way to free myself from the dangerous old cage?

There seemed to be nothing left for me to do but to call for help, in spite of the distrust I felt toward my aunt and cousins, and particularly toward Gabe Guirlande who had not wanted me here any more than had Seena and the others. Were they all involved in some treacherous scheme to be rid of me? Did that explain why whoever had hidden himself on the risers below the second-floor landing, waiting to fling the musty black cloth over my head to blind me, had seemed to possess a force and a strength which was entirely at odds with the ghost woman's emaciated fragility? Had she been merely the bait they had used to lure me? Valerie perhaps, or even Magda, made up to appear chillingly gaunt and ethereal, like a creature from behind the grave? While Gabe, or perhaps Valmir, waited for me near the gate to the old elevator, the velvet shroud spread ready to fling over my head in a gesture designed to terrify me?

I huddled in silence at the bottom of the treacherous cage, chilled by my thoughts. What if I should call out for someone to come to my rescue, only to discover that it was their intention to leave me here, trapped between the mansion's high-ceilinged floors until I died from starvation or exhaustion? The thought was too hideous to be endured and I thrust it aside, telling myself that things like that simply did not happen. Not in real life.

I was able then to call Seena's name, the sound of my voice swiftly dying, swallowed by the mansion's stultifying silence.

I called a second time and waited. In my haste to follow the ghost woman from my room, I had neglected to fling on my robe. Now it occurred to me that, should Gabe or Valmir happen to be the first to hear my calls for help, it might prove to be embarrassing to have one of them find me clad only in my thin nightdress. I reached to wrap the musty length of velvet cloth around my body in an attempt to make myself decently presentable.

But I had moved too quickly. Without warning, the ancient cage began to sway, the frayed ropes groaning ominously beneath the sudden impact of my lightly shifting weight. On a sudden wave of terror, I felt the cage begin slowly to sag even before I heard a wicked little laugh, high above me, followed by the dull snap of a rope breaking.

My hands flew automatically to clutch at the curlicued grille beside me, my senses reeling as the floor of the cage tilted beneath me. Clinging breathlessly to the wrought-iron swirls, I waited for the sickening pendulum motion to cease, half-expecting to go crashing at any moment into the depths of the well.

But by some miracle the ropes attached to the side of the elevator to which I still clung remained secure in their ornate tracks. However, to my dismay, I found when the swinging motions had finally ceased that I could not right myself. The cage hung now at a precarious angle, one side of it tipped treacherously downward so that the benches and floor sloped sharply away from me.

From somewhere above me came the soft sound of impish laughter. Cautiously I strained my neck backward to stare up through the crooked grille, making out a light flutter of movement high above me.

"I warned you to go away," that same whispering voice I had heard before said to me from out of the mansion's shadows. "You can't say I didn't warn you."

"Please. Go find someone to get me out of here," I gasped.

"You're as safe there as you are anywhere in this house," came the whispered reply. "You should have heeded my warning. Instead you tried to follow me, and look where it got you."

"You did this?" I gasped disbelievingly. "You put me here?"

"No! No!" the ghost woman hissed at me in angry protest. "I told Lorainne I would never harm you."

I told Lorainne . . . My mother *had* been here then.

"Who are you?" I cried desperately into the grim shadows above me, where a pale face appeared to hover against an ethereal cloudiness. "Why won't you tell me where Lorainne is now?"

"Amber," came the whispered reply. "Amber. Lorainne recognized me. That's why she had to go away."

Mad. The iron curlicues cut into my clinging hands, turning them numb. I wondered vaguely how much longer I could hold on, as the burning pain inside my head began to worsen, taking up a throbbing cadence. *Mad. Mad. Mad.*

Suddenly it seemed that I was the one who was insane. For I could no longer be certain what it was I had heard or seen, beyond the perimeter of my own wildly rioting senses.

Dazedly I became aware of a light flickering. Lifting my drooping head, I stared upward. A match flared against the darkness above me. For a terrorizing moment, I imagined that it was the ghost woman's intention to drop the small blaze down on me and I visualized with a nightmare clarity the filmy synthetic of my nightdress igniting to turn me into a living torch.

But apparently that was not what she had intended, or if she had, she thought better of it. For in the next instant, a candle guttered, a drop of wax falling onto my bare shoulder, its heat diminished to scarcely more than a warm prickle.

The yellow flame leapt upward, briefly illuminating features that remained indistinguishable, lost as they were between the thick wings of her hair. She leaned above me, across the curving rail, the glow from her candle casting a pattern of darkly dancing shadows onto my upturned face as I continued to stare up at her.

"If you had been Lorainne, everything would have been all right," she said in her soft whispering voice.

"But I'm not," I said weakly.

"For that, you must die if you choose to remain at Blackhurst Hall." She stayed as she was for a moment or two longer, long enough for me to make out the shimmering translucence of her pale shoulders.

Incredibly her arms that had been partially veiled by the black lace folds of the bertha collar when I had seen her earlier had taken on that same ethereal paleness, her flesh appearing now to glow with some eerie luminescence of its own. At the same time her right hand was still hidden from me, as it had been before, except that now it appeared to be lost behind a cloudy white mist, as though, I thought disbelievingly, she had begun slowly to dissipate before my very eyes.

Amber. Was it possible?

She was shielded from me now by a misty whiteness which clung around her like a silvery miasma through which the glow from her candle was visible, the tiny flame leaping like a *feu follet* lost in the mist of a steamy swampland.

Numbly I thought then that I heard a man's voice say softly, "Amber. My angel. My dove."

"Your bride," I heard her whisper faintly.

Only then did I realize that the ghost woman who claimed to be Amber had exchanged the satin-and-lace gown she had worn when I woke to find her in my room for a bridal gown and veil.

Chapter FOURTEEN

I have no idea how long I hung inside the crazily listing elevator waiting for someone to hear my cries.

Dawn was breaking when at last I heard the sound of a door opening and closing, followed by the soft thud of rapidly approaching footsteps in the hallway below me.

I had succeeded at some point during the endlessly dragging night in finding a tentative toehold for my feet. Nevertheless I had not quite dared to let go of the iron scrolls for fear that the least jarring motion might send the old elevator plummeting into the depths of the house.

I suppose that somewhere in the midst of my numbed thoughts had lurked the hope that the ghost woman might eventually return, bringing the man whose voice I had heard speaking to her from beyond the dark curve of the staircase to my rescue. Or had I only imagined that I had heard a man's voice uttering the same flowering sentiments that long-ago bride had set down in her diary? Was it Charles Blackhurst's voice I had heard, coming to me from out of Blackhurst Hall's stormy past? And what of the ghost woman who had appeared in my room wearing amber satin and black lace, only to materialize a short while later clad shimmeringly in bridal white? Had I somehow managed to conjure her with an imagination that had become overtaxed by my concern for my missing mother, taking my cues from the old trunk whose contents I had so eagerly examined?

I peered down helplessly between wrought-iron tulips and poppies and stiffly twining ivy, no longer certain of anything I saw or heard. Did I dare to trust my feverish senses now, when they told me that someone was coming at last to save me?

"Please," I whimpered, sounding more like a lost puppy than a girl who needed saving.

It was Gabe who appeared below me, his dark face an unreadable mask as he leaned over winding banister to stare up at me.

"Tracey! In God's name, what do you think you're doing?" He uttered a curse, vanishing before I could find my voice to answer him.

I heard his footsteps rushing swiftly away

from me, down the spiraling staircase. After what seemed yet another eon, I felt the cage sway gently on its frayed ropes.

Then slowly, so slowly that I was not certain at first that it had moved at all, the elevator began to descend, the pulleys above me groaning in screeching protest as the thready ropes began slowly to crawl across their dry wheels.

"You little fool!" Gabe said, when at last the elevator arrived at the ground floor. He jerked open the grilled door with an angry clang. "Seena told you not to go near this thing; I heard her myself. Yet apparently you wasted no time in beelining straight into what could very well have proved to be your deathtrap."

Deathtrap. His unfortunate choice of words rattled with a shattering cadence through my pain-numbed thoughts. I felt weak and dizzy. But I would not let him see how shaken I was.

I said, forcing my voice to stay steady, in spite of the pounding pain which thundered behind my ears with a jarring force, "Do you think I would have gone into that monstrosity on my own?"

"At the moment, I'm not certain what I think," he said gruffly. "How long have you been dangling up there, for God's sake?"

He paused to measure me with his fierce stare, his expression unchanging as he took in my flimsy nightdress that I had forgotten I was wearing until now. "The least you could have done was to put on some clothes before you set off on your little adventure." In a single sweeping motion, he pulled off his shirt and wrapped it around me. "Get your arms into this before someone sees you and thinks the worst about us." I could not tell whether he was serious or whether he had resumed his consummate air of cynicism.

I said, a wave of frustration and anger sweeping over me, "You're treating me as if I were a child. I *didn't* disobey Seena, as you so gallantly put it. I was pushed into that ancient cage against my will. Here, feel for yourself." I reached impulsively for his hand, pressing his palm against the throbbing lump at the side of my head.

"So you fell down and went bump in the night," he said maddeningly, his fingers tangling in my hair. "I'm surprised it isn't worse than that, considering the condition of that elevator. Don't you realize that you might have been killed, had that thing come crashing all the way down with you? Seena had good reason to warn you. A woman once had her back . . ."

218

I cut him off, not wanting to hear. "I called for someone to come to my rescue when I first realized where I was," I said. "That must have been hours ago. And you are only just now getting here," I added unfairly.

He looked at me, the cynicism that had darkened his face a moment before disappearing. He looked very fierce then. "The walls in this house are two feet thick. The next time you decide to take your life into your hands, make certain first that I've left my door ajar."

"You don't believe me, do you?" I said, my knees suddenly trembling.

I went to the stairs, sinking onto the bottom step.

"If someone *did* push you into that thing, you must have made it easy for him," he conceded.

"It wasn't a he . . ." I broke off, alerted by something in his expression, thinking then that he had pictured me with Valmir. "In any case, I choose to live my life differently from the way you choose to live yours," I went on recklessly.

"How can you possibly know *how* I choose to live my life?" he countered. "And if you are thinking that I imagined you were with Valmir, well, those are your sentiments, not mine."

"Why should you even have said such a thing to me if it wasn't what you were thinking?" I said accusingly.

"Perhaps because I know Valmir far better than you do," he said with a maddening calm.

"At least he's a gentleman," I challenged.

He chose to ignore me. "However you came to be inside this mantrap, it won't happen again," he said gruffly.

Taking a knife from the pocket of his jeans, he snapped open the blade and began to slash through the ropes that looped down from the top of the cage like thickly coiling snakes.

I watched him uncertainly, seeing the tightly corded muscles rippling smoothly along his bare arms, more acutely aware of his lean strength and vigor than I wanted to be.

Had it been Gabe who had assumed a disguise to resemble that first bride named Amber? But that was preposterous.

At the same time, I could not discredit the fact that whoever had lain in wait for me near the second-floor landing had been strong. Strong enough to fling me backward when he or she had tossed the musty square of velvet cloth over my head and to lift my unconscious body into the elevator cage after I had fallen beneath the force of that onslaught.

The length of black velvet . . . I wondered why I had not thought of it sooner. It would serve as the evidence I needed to prove to Gabe Guirlande's objectively legal mind that I had been attacked after all.

Rising carefully from the step to avoid jarring my throbbing head any more than was necessary, I went to look for the dark cloth inside the cage. But it was no longer there. It occurred to me then that it must have slipped between the iron grilles when the elevator tilted sideways and was no doubt lying beneath the cage at this very moment so that there seemed to be no chance that I might retrieve it.

On impulse, I went then to examine the ropes on the side of the cage opposite Gabe, who looked up from the severed ropes he had bundled into his hands to watch me, his expression seeming to suggest that he thought me thoroughly mad.

"Haven't you had enough of this thing?" he asked curiously. "Or has it become an obsession of some kind with you?"

"I'm searching for evidence," I said, suddenly aware of how ridiculous I must appear to him, clad in the long, thin gown which clung statically to my legs below the hem of his shirt.

"What kind of evidence?" he asked.

"Slashed ropes," I said.

"Why should you imagine that someone had cut the ropes?" His voice was that of an attorney conducting a cross-examination.

"Because I heard a wicked little laugh when the cage let go," I flung at him recklessly, not certain now that I had heard anything at all.

What if the length of black velvet was not there beneath the cage, as I wanted to believe it was? What if I was more deeply affected by the old house with its dark hints of mystery and intrigue than I had so far realized? I bent to run my fingers along the base of the cage. But there was nothing there. Nothing at all.

"You saw who it was that laughed at you?" he was saying.

"Not actually," I was forced to admit. "Whoever it was threw a sheet over my head before she pushed me into the elevator and ran back up the stairs."

I paused. The stooping motion had triggered afresh the throbbing pain behind my temple. I reached to clutch the iron grille beside me to keep from swaying.

"And you were dragged, struggling all the while, from your room to the elevator well," he said skeptically, still the attorney attempting to discredit my testimony.

"It wasn't like that at all," I said, still holding to the side of the cage.

"But you've just told me . . ."

I cut him off, my voice verging suddenly on tears. "Whoever it was lured me to the elevator well first. Then when I wasn't looking, she . . . he threw a dark cloth over my head. It was thick and black and musty. Velvet, I think. Which is why I was unable to scream, if that was to be your next question."

"The cloth . . . where is it now?" He made a pretense of searching the floor of the cage, glancing up to give me a gallic shrug when he failed to find anything.

"You say you were lured," he continued before I could explain my theory about the missing cloth.

"She came to my room," I said. "I woke to find her standing inside the doorway, watching me through the mosquito *barre*." I hesitated, my head throbbing abominably so that I could no longer be certain whether or not my story made sense.

Story. Waves of doubt washed over me. Was that all it amounted to? Yet another

223

morbid little tale to add to the house's long list of unprovable legends?

"You got a look at her face?" Gabe was asking me, his expression suddenly guarded.

I managed a dull little nod. "It . . . it wasn't a normal face," I heard myself saying. "She wore a dress I had seen earlier in the attic. She wanted me to believe she was . . . someone else," I ended lamely, unable to bring myself to tell him that I had seen a ghost.

"You're not making sense, you know," Gabe said quietly. "I think it might be a good idea if I were to call Dr. Whitaker out from town to have a look at you." His fierce stare bored into me.

I opened my mouth to speak. But no sound came. Suddenly there was only the pain, throbbing behind my temple with a fearful intensity. I moved dizzily toward the stairs.

But I had waited too long. A cold black wave had started to sweep over me and even as I began to fall, I found myself thinking, "For the first time in my life, I am going to faint . . ."

When I came to, Gabe was bending over me.

"Just lie quietly. It's all right. Everything is all right." He pressed something cold and wet against my brow.

"But it's not," I whispered. "It's not all right at all."

"It will be," he said, his long arms swooping to gather me up off the hard floor.

I tried to struggle but there was no way I could break away from him. Holding me tightly, he went with me up the stairs, carrying me as effortlessly as if I had been a child.

Chapter FIFTEEN

By the time I was ready to go down to dinner that evening, I had made up my mind to ask about Amber. Clearly Gabe had not wanted to believe me when I had told him that someone wearing a gown from the mansion's attic had appeared in the doorway to my room to lure me into the hallway in the direction of the old elevator. Furthermore he had not bothered to conceal his skepticism when I told him how I came to be trapped inside the ancient cage, high above the ground floor.

Nor had the doctor he had called to examine my bruises found anything out of the ordinary which could serve to corroborate my story. The blow I had received was not serious, Dr. Whitaker told me, his assumption being that I had tripped on the stairs and had fallen and struck my head against the ornately scrolled gate of the old elevator. I guessed then that that was what Gabe had told him over the phone. Although I had wanted then to tell him the truth as I remembered it, when I turned my head on the goosedown pillow to find Gabe watching from the shadows beyond my open doorway, I had not quite dared to speak.

Now, as I paused before the gilt-framed mirror above the marble-topped dresser to put the finishing touches on my makeup in an attempt to hide my pallor, I could not help wondering what Gabe's reaction might have been had I told him everything when he first found me, hanging precariously inside the elevator cage, high above the comparative safety of the ground level of the house. Would he have been more inclined to believe my story had I mentioned Amber's name in conjunction with the chilling series of events that had overtaken me? Who besides myself and my mother had looked into the old trunk to find her diary? Gabe? Was he involved in some intricate scheme to frighten me away from Blackhurst Hall before my grandfather's missing will could be found?

Try as I might, I could not free myself from a growing suspicion that Gabe Guirlande was determined to claim a share of the plantation's vastly sprawling sugar lands. In which case, he could have nothing to fear from me. Unless, I thought chillingly, he was in some way responsible

227

for my mother's disappearance and dreaded what I might find. He alone among those who lived in the old house knew that I had taken it upon myself to search not only the overseer's office but the ballroom attic. I had given myself away when I had told him that the woman who had appeared in my room had been wearing a gown I had seen in the attic earlier.

Had he in some way harmed my mother? Was she dead? The thought came unbidden to my mind, sending a cold wave of apprehension through me.

Gathering up the brightly patterned folds of my floor-length dinner gown, I turned away from my own frightened face to go quickly down the stairs, my mind whirling in an effort to decide how best to broach the subject of the long-ago bride whose ghost could find no rest.

I suppose the thought was in the back of my mind that whoever was responsible for the frightening events following my mother's mysterious disappearance would somehow give himself away when I brought Amber's name into the conversation. In any case, I had a compelling need to know more about that first bride if only because I could no longer be certain of what I had seen and heard in this house, with its dark, shifting shadows and strange noises.

When I entered the dining room, Gabe was standing at a marble-topped sideboard fixing a drink for Magda. He smiled his crooked little smile as he caught sight of me, breaking off what he had been saying to ask me how I felt.

"I'm fine now," I said guardedly.

"Except for a classic case of burning ears, I suspect," Magda interjected candidly.

"We were discussing your accident," Seena said from her place beside the double doors, which had been flung wide to admit the light breeze stirring the garden.

"Either you are far braver than you look or a sleepwalker, one of the two," Magda persisted, her black gaze piercing me. "Or were you on your way to keep a liaison when you became trapped inside that dreadful old cage?"

My cheeks burned when I saw the look that had come onto her face; a look which said all too clearly that it was the sort of thing she expected from Lorainne O'Toole's daughter.

I said coldly, "If you don't mind, I prefer not to discuss it." I looked at their faces carefully, hoping to find some clue which

229

would tell me what Gabe had said to them concerning my so-called accident.

"Perhaps a drink will help," said Valmir.

He leaned casually inside the doorjamb, a half-empty glass tilted rakishly in his hand, while Valerie sat near him on the floor, the red velvet cushion beneath her making a bright splash against the polished boards.

"What will it be, Tracey?" Gabe pulled his gaze away from me to hand Magda an on-the-rocks stemmed glass with the letter B etched into its amber crystal. "Brandy? A cold bourbon toddy?"

"A Sazerac, I think," I said, aware that Magda watched me.

Even though I was not quite certain what the drink I had once heard my father refer to as the most celebrated of New Orleans cocktails consisted of, I experienced the gratifying sensation of having achieved a coup of sorts when I saw surprise glitter briefly behind her black eyes.

"We aren't exactly Bourbon Street here, although I expect Gabe can manage with what there is," Magda said in her sultry drawl. "Although I must say, you surprise me, Tracey. You don't look the whiskey-and-bitters type at all. I should think a Shirley Temple or a Horse's Neck might suit you better, if you'd care to reconsider before Gabe becomes involved with all of that messiness of rinsing glasses in absinthe and measuring sugar."

"If it's too much trouble . . ." I hesitated, feeling suddenly trapped by her.

I had the sudden thought then that regardless of what I had asked Gabe to fix for me, she would have found a way to belittle me for it.

I was certain of it when she went on in that same scathingly superior way, "Well? I suppose you've decided now that you must have a Roffignac or something equally unheard of."

"Sazerac it is," Gabe said pleasantly, choosing to ignore her efforts to involve me in her absurdly challenging little contretemps.

Turning quickly away from her, I went to join the others near the open doorway.

"You look stunning tonight," Valmir said to me. "A trifle wan, perhaps. But ravishing nonetheless. You are really a very beautiful girl, Tracey. But then what else could one expect of Lorainne's daughter," he added obscurely.

"You remember what she looked like," I said quickly.

"It hasn't been that long ago since she

last visited here," Valmir said smoothly.

I became aware of the glowering look Valerie had turned on me, her small, pointed face tilted upward toward Valmir like the brown-velvet face of a pansy turning toward the sun.

"Frankly I don't remember her all that well and, I strongly suspect, neither does Valmir. I wouldn't be taken in by him if I were you," she added, perching like a pixie on her red pillow, her reed-slim body svelte in a white jersey halter and long, bikini-style skirt slit to the thigh to show stunning expanses of sun-toasted skin.

Valmir, as I might have expected, was also in white, his open shirt revealing a dangling St. Christopher surrounded by small, glittering stones.

Seena, I noticed, looked remarkably cool and collected in a lime-green caftan which exactly matched the color of the daiquiri she held in her hand. I saw then that her fingers trembled slightly, in contrast to the smooth composure of her face. It was as though she were striving to hold some deeply jarring emotion sternly in check and had not quite succeeded.

"Perhaps you'd care to tell me why you went into the elevator when I specifically warned you against going there," my aunt said when she saw me looking at her. She spoke softly, her voice guarded as though she did not want the others to hear.

I tried to think of some logical reason why I might have gone there, apart from the truth, which I was more certain than ever none of them were prepared to accept, including my aunt.

"Does it really matter now?" I finally said when nothing came to me.

"Perhaps not," she said.

But I could not help noticing that her voice was guarded, her eyes continuing to question me, as though, I thought, she were attempting to convince herself that my unfortunate mishap had indeed been the accident Gabe must have described for her behind my back.

"Here's your Sazerac, Tracey," Gabe said at my elbow.

I turned, seeing for the first time the portrait above the mantel. It was the portrait of a young woman, her hair the color of amber honey. She was wearing a dress of amber satin cut low over her shoulders, the soft, white shimmer of her pale flesh gleaming through the ornate black lace of a wide bertha collar.

For a moment or two, I imagined that I was going mad. Taking the glass Gabe handed me, I raised its rim to my lips, the portrait commanding me.

It wasn't a large painting. Nor would I have been quite so apt to notice it had I not been standing across from it at an angle, half-hidden as it was behind the polished globe of a tall, lighthouse shelf clock.

Even so, there was no mistaking the gown the girl in the painting wore, and I went with my drink to peer behind the clock's crystal globe in an effort to see her features more clearly. Half-turned so that she had not been facing the artist, her painted stare seemed uncannily to follow me as I approached the high marble mantle.

"She was Blackhurst's first bride," Gabe said at my shoulder.

In the next instant, Seena gave a strangled little cry. I saw when I turned startled eyes on her that her face had turned chalky.

"What is it, Mother?" Valmir knelt beside her chair, reaching to chafe her trembling fingers.

"Are you responsible for this . . . this outrage?" My aunt gestured wildly in the direction of the painting, her stare going accusingly to Magda. "You know how I've always hated that . . . vixenish likeness."

"But I thought you must have been the one who asked Henri to bring it down from the attic," Magda replied, coming to stand between Gabe and me, her gaze drawn to the portrait as mine was. "Really, I don't see what all the fuss is about. It's high time the poor thing was brought out of hiding."

Unappeased, Seena turned her accusing stare on Valerie. "Had you something to do with this?" she demanded in tones which were more outraged than angry.

"Of course not." Valerie stared steadily up into Seena's face, a look that I could not read passing between them.

Almost visibly Seena's slight body appeared to shrink inside her cleverly styled caftan, something that I recognized as fear moving swiftly across her face so that her small features seemed suddenly to freeze into a carefully controlled mask.

It was Valmir who said, giving Seena one of his warmly winning smiles, "I'm certain there's some logical reason why the painting is there. In any case, I'll take it back to the attic after we've finished dinner."

"Would you, darling?" Seena said in a small, grateful voice which seemed to suggest that, of them all, Valmir alone knew how to please her.

Only then did I dare to say of the painting, "Whether she belongs here or not, I find her fascinating."

"She was a . . . a trollop," Seena ended lamely. There was falseness in her voice which made me uneasy.

"She looks respectable enough to me," Gabe commented. "She was, after all, a Creole of good breeding, educated at the convent in New Orleans."

"And her name?" I said, although there was no real need for me to ask.

"*Ambre*," Gabe said.

The eyes of the girl in the portrait seemed suddenly to mock me.

Chapter SIXTEEN

I said, feeling only slightly guilty as I feigned an innocence I did not have, "Which of my ancestors did Amber marry?"

It was Valmir who said, "Charles. Charles Blackhurst, a man I have always admired. Not only did he have a knack for accumulating riches, but he knew how to savor life to the fullest."

"Obviously he had excellent taste when it came to women," Gabe said, gazing appreciatively at the beauty in the painting. "I've always wondered what the heroine of that curious old legend looked like."

"Apparently you aren't the least bit disappointed," Magda observed drily. "Had I known you preferred redheads, darling, I should have had my tresses stripped and dyed long before this."

"You mentioned a legend," I said, scarcely able to curb my impatience with Magda's awkward flirtations, which seemed oddly out of character when I glanced down to see the ivory-handled whip in her hand, half-hidden behind the folds of her flowing, gypsy skirt.

"I don't suppose Lorainne ever got around to telling you about Amber," Magda said.

She watched me curiously, as if to find something in my face which would tell her how much I knew.

I said, not quite truthfully, "If she did, I've forgotten what it was."

"It's not the sort of thing a mother tells her daughter," Seena said disapprovingly.

"The truth is, Tracey, that our ancestor, Charles Blackhurst, committed a slight indiscretion when he brought Amber to this house," Magda commented.

I remembered the entries I had read in Amber's diary, and I became more curious than ever about the girl who smiled down coquettishly from above the mantle.

I said, not without a grain of truth, "I seem to recall something about his having had a mistress."

Seena gave me a shocked stare. "If Lorainne told you that, she is even more indiscreet than I had imagined."

"Things have changed since then," I said defensively. "No one thinks twice now about couples who live together before they are married."

"This is still the Deep South, darling,"

Magda drawled. "I've an idea you've given Mother a thorough jar with your advocacy of free love."

"I don't consider that the sort of thing a mother tells her daughter, no matter how much the times have changed since Charles Blackhurst brought his . . . his *fille à la cassette* into this house."

"The *filles à la cassette* were before Amber's time," Gabe said. He looked at me. "In case you're wondering, they were French peasant girls who were brought by the French government to the Ursuline Convent in New Orleans, where the nuns cared for them until a marriage could be arranged for them with one of the French soldiers stationed there. The soldiers were given their discharge, a plot of land, provisions, a rifle, and a cow when their choice was made. The girl's dowry consisted of whatever she had brought with her to this country in her casket, which accounts for the name that was used to describe them. They were all girls who were alone in the world, either orphaned or living in the asylums of Paris," he added. "Ambre Aurore Lestant was none of those things."

I felt my heart begin to pound. Had Gabe read Amber's diary as I had done?

Did that explain how he came to know so much about her?

I said, "It would be difficult to imagine a simple peasant girl becoming mistress of this huge house."

"Amber was never actually mistress here," Magda said. "Poor thing," she added when I shot her a curious look.

"Amber became mysteriously ill on the day of her wedding to Charles Blackhurst," Gabe said quietly. "So ill, as a matter of fact, that she was thought to be dead. The unfortunate thing is, they buried her."

"But I don't understand," I said, a strange little chill going over me.

"Alive, darling. Amber was buried alive," Magda said, turning to the table to take a slender black cigar from the gold case which lay beside her plate.

"How dreadful!" I whispered.

"Yes it was, wasn't it," Valmir remarked, while Valerie maintained her sullen silence, sitting poised with a queer, nervous watch-fulness beside Seena's chair.

"It's my theory that she was a victim of catalepsy," Gabe said. "There's no way to prove it, of course. Not at this late date. But all of the pieces seem to fit."

"I take it she was rescued," I said. "Be-fore . . . before she really did die," I added

240

with a little shudder.

"That's what's so dreadful," Seena said in a small, trembling voice. "There was no way to save her. No way at all."

Valerie's face was suddenly drained of all color. "There's no way for us to know that either. Not now," she said quickly, reaching to lay a protective hand on Seena's arm.

Seena started, as if she had been absorbed by her own morbid thoughts. "She is dead, isn't she," she remarked in a vague voice. Whether she intended them to or not, her words held a questioning inflection.

The air of conspiracy I had sensed around me in the old house seemed deeper somehow, the people who lived here more desperately affected by its tragic old legends than I had first imagined.

I said quickly, "But if she were saved, at least for the immediate moment, I should think that would have somehow alleviated the tragic circumstances of her wedding day. And catalepsy must have been recognizable even then, so they would not have been apt to bury her alive if it had happened to her a second time. Unless it was one of those dread things they locked people away for, imagining them to be insane," I added on impulse.

"I suppose it's common knowledge now that catalepsy is a condition associated with mental illness," Gabe commented, going to replenish his empty glass at the bar. "It's mostly found in catatonic schizophrenia, as I understand it. The patient — in this case, Amber — goes into a trance-like or stuporous state and the body becomes rigid. It's easy to imagine how the ill-informed might mistake such a state for the rigor mortis which invariably sets in a few hours after death. Amber's wasn't an isolated case by any means. There have been numerous other instances of live burial both before and since."

"Amber revived just in the nick of time, I take it," I said, my gaze drawn again to the girl in the painting.

There was something about her eyes, something just a little mad, I thought, as if the artist had glimpsed that darkly shadowed side to her character which had eventually drawn her in upon herself.

"Unfortunately no," Gabe said.

"But she was dead, we must believe that," Seena said from her chair beside the open doorway.

Then I saw her face, chalky white in the shadows beyond the perimeter of light cast by the tinkling chandelier hanging above the silver-and-china-laden table Odalie had laid before we came down. Valerie made a swift motion to take her half-finished daiquiri from fingers that had begun suddenly to tremble.

Gabe appeared to be too deeply involved with his story to take note of Seena's horrified reaction, his voice saying quietly beside me, "Her casket was put into the tomb Charles Blackhurst had built behind the sugar house when his first wife died. It must have been a painful time for him, considering the big splash he had made of the wedding. He'd brought in some kind of monstrous spiders from China to spin their webs in the trees around the house. The slaves had gilded the webs with gold and silver and there were canvases spread for dancing. One of Blackhurst's wealthy Creole neighbors, a man by the name of Charles Durande, had put on a similar show for one of his daughters, and I suppose, since Amber had been his ward before he eventually decided to marry her, Blackhurst felt it was the least he could do."

"You can imagine how his grown sons and daughters reacted to all of that extravagance for a girl who was already his mistress," Valmir commented.

"I know what I should have done had I

been one of them," Magda stated.

"Vengeful creature that you are, you'd have murdered the poor girl no doubt," Valmir said drily.

"How do we know that isn't precisely what happened?" Magda retorted. "It would have been a simple matter for one of them to slip poison into her glass during the reception. The champagne must have flowed like water. And she was, after all, a usurper." Magda's inscrutable black eyes darted me a fiery look, her mouth twisting into a treacherous little smile. "Which of our theories do you prefer, Tracey? Mine or Gabe's?"

"I can tell that better when I've heard the end of the story," I said.

"That same night, after Amber's supposed remains had been laid to rest in the vault, her distraught bridegroom heard a peculiar crawling noise, after he had retired," Gabe continued. "According to the legend — and you have to remember that is all it amounts to — an incident which became embroidered out of all proportion with each consecutive telling — the sounds seemed to come to him from the brick-paved gallery. A violent thunderstorm had risen by then, and Charles Blackhurst marked the noises off to some idiosyncrasy of the wind."

"I can picture him going onto the gallery outside his bedroom to stare at all those gilded webs flying wildly off into the night," Valerie said, her pointed face becoming strangely animated. "The Negroes would have been wailing in their quarters, lighting their charm lamps and invoking their Voodoo gods to save massa and themselves from certain destruction."

"There were others who heard sounds that night," Gabe said. "One of the house Negroes claimed to have seen a pale form gliding through the rain-drenched gardens, but he didn't tell anyone until after they had found her the following morning."

"Don't look so hopeful, Tracey," Magda warned. "I don't like to shatter whatever romantic fancies you're having just now. But the poor thing was dead. They found her lifeless body resting against one of the front columns of the house. She'd been buried with her jewels, and someone had used the amber necklace she was wearing to strangle her. It was found knotted into a hangman's noose about her neck. As if that were not reason enough for her to be dead by then — truly dead — her right hand had been severed."

A nightmare sensation wrenched through me, and for a dizzying moment I thought I would faint. Then, as I became aware of Gabe watching me, his look telling me that he was thinking of the beads he had seen me put into my pocket, I felt the color coming back into my cheeks.

I said, "I suppose you are going to tell me next that one of Charles Blackhurst's sons or daughters did it when they realized that Amber might pose some kind of threat to their security as his heirs."

"One of the menservants confessed," Gabe said. "He had gone to Amber's grave to rob it of her jewels. He was attempting to remove her rings when she suddenly revived. Knowing how superstitious the blacks were, you can imagine the poor fellow's terror. He knotted the amber necklace tightly around her neck in an attempt to silence what he must have imagined by then to be her spirit rising up to seek its revenge. But in his panic he didn't knot it tightly enough. When he couldn't remove her rings, he severed her hand and made off with his terrible trophy, leaving the poor girl alone in that deplorable condition. Evidently the pain of having her hand severed rallied her enough to enable her to crawl from the tomb to the mansion before she died from a loss of blood."

"The slave who was responsible paid for

his crime, of course," Valmir said. "Charles Blackhurst had him whipped to death by the black who served as his overseer, with the entire slave community standing witness. I suspect it was a lesson none of them ever forgot."

I forced myself to speak. "As dastardly as his crime was, I'm surprised Charles Blackhurst didn't attend to the whipping himself."

"You're forgetting that our ancestor was a gentleman-planter," Valmir said. "Can you imagine *me* taking whip in hand to beat some poor sniveling slave to death? Magda, yes. It's something she would accomplish with relish."

"Nevertheless, Charles Blackhurst was the target for his curse," Valerie said, her small, vixenish face sulky behind its shimmering suntan. She looked at Gabe. "You've skipped over that part of the story. You may as well tell Tracey the rest of it, now that you've gone this far."

"Frankly I don't hold much with curses," Gabe said. "Although I suppose it does add a certain fillip to the story."

I searched his face for some sign which would tell me what he was really thinking behind his arrogant Cajun facade. But if it had been his deliberate intention to skip over that part of the story for some secret reason of his own, I could not tell.

"Local lore has it that the slave who was whipped to death for his desecration of Amber's grave and her subsequent demise used his last breath to utter an obeah incantation of some kind," he continued. "The gist of it seems to be that he doomed Amber's spirit to haunt Blackhurst Hall and its occupants forevermore." He gave me a grim little smile. "Curses seem to be typical of tales of this kind."

"Odalie used that malevolent tidbit to frighten us into being good when we were small," Valmir said, his smile seeming suddenly a little strained. "I was always looking around me for ghosts in this old pile."

"There are plenty of those," Magda remarked. She flashed me one of her obscure looks. "Including Amber's, of course. There are those who still hear her crawling about out there on those moldy old bricks that pave the gallery's floor."

I found myself casting a quick, nervous look toward the front of the house.

"I shall never forgive Odalie for using that hideous nonsense to frighten you behind my back," Seena said with surprising vehemence.

"I doubt that it affected any of us that

248

deeply," Magda said.

"Look what it's done to your sister!" Seena said.

"If you are referring to Valerie's obsession with the occult, witches are born, not made," Magda replied, her stare burning now into Seena, as though, I thought, she were attempting to warn her.

What were they hiding from me, I thought, as we went then to the long dining table. Why did they keep the west wing locked against me? And what of the trunk I had found in the attic; who kept Amber's clothes so perfectly folded?

Who had worn the amber satin, only to exchange it later for a bridal gown and veil?

And, more important, why?

Chapter SEVENTEEN

Unable to sleep, haunted by the tragic tale Gabe had told me, I slipped into my robe and went out through the French windows onto the gallery.

The moon hung like a huge, silvery disk behind the moss-hung live oaks and the giant pecan trees stretching in a thick, dark wall to form the alley. Wisps of ground mist wound through the garden like ragged ribbons, the sultry perfumes of the blossoming shrubs rising in a thick mixture to crowd my senses.

A queer, aching nostalgia flooded through me. Where was my mother, I thought. Where had she gone and why?

I could not help thinking then of the ghost woman who had mistaken me for Lorainne when she had appeared in my room the previous evening. *Amber.* There was no longer the least doubt in my mind that whoever had assumed that chilling role was determined to frighten me away from Blackhurst, perhaps even to kill me. Had my mother been warned to leave in that same terrifying manner, I wondered. Did that explain why she had disappeared so mysteriously? Why else should the ghost woman have imagined, when she saw me lying behind the misty folds of the mosquito *barre,* that Lorainne had returned to her?

More deeply affected than I wanted to be by the legend Gabe had related, I decided that if I were to have the answers I needed, I must double my efforts to find some evidence which would prove conclusively that my mother had been here far more recently than either Seena or my cousins were willing to admit. Only then would I dare to confront them and demand of them that they tell me where she was.

As it was, I felt powerless to act, more convinced than ever that not only my aunt and cousins but Gabe Guirlande as well were involved in some tacit conspiracy to drive me away. And if I did not go, as the ghost woman had told me to do, what then?

But I would not think of that now. Not until I had succeeded in finding the proof I needed to show me where my mother had gone and why.

Somewhere a mockingbird trilled and

from farther away came the same soft hoot I had heard before, rising above the raucous cadence of the nearby swamps. Owls, snakes, frogs, and buzzards were all in league with the spirits of night. My mother had told me that. Spiders, too, spinning their clinging webs behind the vines, so that I felt a faintly moist viscosity touch my forehead when I turned to reach for the handle of the window.

It was then that I saw a flicker of light, scarcely more than a bright pinpoint touching the velvet blackness below me. I moved back to the rail to peer between the vines. A match flared, the tiny tongue of orange flame licking at the wall of darkness in a far corner of the garden. I could not tell how far away it was, somewhere beyond the ancient *garçonnière* which stood opposite the west wing, I thought, thinking too of the ghost woman with her dimly flaring candle.

I hesitated. Then I whirled about, hurried out through my room, into the hallway, and down the stairs. This time she would not escape me. This time I would confront her before she could flee back to her hiding place in the west wing. I would demand that she tell me everything she knew concerning my mother's strange disappearance.

Which of them was it, I wondered, glimpsing Valmir through the double doors of the deserted dining room as I made my way across the brick-paved gallery onto a path which would take me to the far side of the house where I had seen the light.

Not Valmir, but perhaps Magda. Would it prove to be my whip-carrying cousin who had struck the match I had seen to touch its flaming tip to one of the evil-looking little cigars which were apparently an addiction of hers? Had she gone into the garden with Gabe? When we had finished the *café royales* he made for us after dinner, he had announced that he was going to the "quarters" to speak with the hands before he retired. I had seen him starting off on the path which led past the old summer kitchen and the overseer's office in the direction of the renovated slave cabins. A moment later Magda had hurried to join him, their bodies lightly touching as they went together into the velvet darkness beyond the pale glow cast by the insect lanterns Seena had asked Henri to light for us on the back gallery.

Pale splashes of moonlight fell in ghostly pools around my feet, as I brushed between lilies and cape jasmine bushes.

I passed by an ancient summer house,

lost behind tangles of honeysuckle and Cherokee roses, their clustered blooms transformed by the moonlight into a multitude of tiny, watching faces.

Ahead of me, the *garçonnière* loomed suddenly from behind banks of camellia bushes. I was nearing the place where I had seen the pinpoint of fire burning against the shadowy darkness beneath the moss-misted live oaks. Pausing in the shadow of the *garçonnière*, I listened, sniffing the air around me for a hint of the cigar smoke which would serve to tell me that it was Magda who had struck the match I saw.

When I neither heard nor smelled anything, beyond the droning sounds from the swamp and the thickly cloying scent of honeysuckle and roses, I went stealthily around the two-story building which had once served to house the plantation's rakish young heirs, providing them with a setting apart from the main house for their bachelor parties and whatever nocturnal forays they might have been inclined to pursue. In spite of Seena's shocked outrage concerning Amber's morals, I was not so naive as to imagine that my ancestors' lives had been quite so prim and proper as she seemed to imagine. There would have been no need for the *garçonnières* which flanked the mansion at either side had they been. The whole idea behind the remote, pagoda-shaped dwellings had been to protect the genteel sensitivities of the planters' daughters from any hint of masculine crassness and vulgarity.

It was the kind of custom Valmir would have enjoyed, I found myself thinking as I skirted behind the tall, octagonal building. Although it was nothing short of ludicrous even to imagine that either Magda or Valerie were of such a delicate turn of mind that it might be deemed necessary to shield them from any knowledge of whatever male indulgences he enjoyed. Fleetingly I wondered if my fourth cousin whom, I vaguely recalled, had been the eldest, had served as their archetype before she died. *Rhea,* Seena had called her. Would she have followed Gabe into the night as Magda had done, her eagerness to claim him painfully obvious? Even though I could detect no smell from Magda's cigar, I had succeeded in convincing myself that she was the one I would find when I reached the corner of the garden where I had seen the flaring match. Magda and Gabe.

Depressed by the thought of seeing the

two of them together, I considered turning back. At the same time, I was filled with a desperate need to find the ghost woman, more certain than ever that she alone among those who lived in the house was the one most apt to tell me what I needed to know concerning my missing mother. If she was somehow demented, as I had come to believe, it was possible that she might tell me far more than any of them intended for me to know.

The thought of both Gabe and the ghost woman filled me with a multitude of ambiguities. I was as frightened of one as I was of the other, I thought, my apprehension growing as I neared the deep shadow cast by the monolithic old trees which had served as a backdrop for the brief flame I had seen from the second-story gallery. Suddenly it seemed an impossible task I had set for myself, when I considered the size of the immediate grounds around the house. *Six acres of exotic trees and shrubbery,* my mother had once told me, *of oak and sweet gum and bay and magnolia.*

Although I could not make out the individual trees and shrubs that surrounded me, I was able to recognize an occasional scent. Lemon and orange trees in bloom . . . and magnolia fuscata. My mother had taken me to the botanical gardens as a child to identify them for me and I had never forgotten.

Now I caught another smell, like hair burning. The acrid stench twined itself around me and I pushed past rows of prickly-stemmed roses to follow it.

I had gone only a short distance when I saw the light. Incredibly now it burned high in the branches of a mammoth live oak. I stared at it disbelievingly, thinking numbly that it was far too strong and bright to be a firefly.

Then I saw her, a pale form clinging dizzily to the thick limb beside the small flickering flame, her face lost to me behind the waving strands of moss which draped around her like a ghostly shroud.

I took a step forward, crouching low in the midst of giant elephant ears and Spanish dagger, peering up past tall spires of waxy blossoms that glimmered like silver bells in the colorless night.

What I had imagined at first to be a lamp or perhaps a candle, mounted in some mysterious way in the heights of the tree, was in actuality a bottle, its lighted wick casting a pale orange glow which was quickly absorbed by the draping strands of gray moss.

There was a sudden sharp movement in the midst of the thickly leafed branches, followed by a queer little thudding sound. In that same instant, I made out the black tail of a whip reaching to twine itself briefly around the burning bottle, which began slowly to sway.

A moment later, the flame inside the bottle licked higher as the crouching figure high in the tree dripped some pale liquid into it from a second container.

"Manman moin . . ." A softly familiar voice intoned to the dancing flames.

My mother . . . What did it mean? A cold wave of dread swept over me, as I continued to watch and to listen.

"Ou pâlé, Tracey *pas couté,"* the voice said.

I realized with a sharp sense of dread that it belonged to my cousin Valerie. Cautiously I shifted my position in the midst of the rustling leaves in an effort to see her more clearly, making out the brief whiteness of her halter above her low-slung skirt. Because she was so deeply tanned, I could not see her face clearly. Yet I knew how it must look, her black eyes burning with a sultry fire in the midst of her piquant features which wore a perpetual look of displeasure.

"You speak, Tracey don't listen," she said this time in English. *"Se dépêcher aller! Poussez aller,* Tracey O'Toole!" she spat fiercely.

Although I could not translate her Cajun patois accurately, I guessed that she was repeating some ancient Voodoo chant, nor did I need to understand it clearly to know what she was saying: *Make haste and go! Hurry and go, Tracey O'Toole!*

Go away! Go away! the ghost woman had whispered to me. Had that low, warning voice belonged to Valerie? Had it been her intention first to frighten me away from Blackhurst Hall by pretending to be Amber's ghost? And when that had failed to work, had she decided then to resort to some weird, occult practice in an effort to be rid of me?

"I call upon thee, Pethro loa, at the midnight hour; the hour of evil," my cousin chanted, oblivious to my watching presence in the moon-shadowed garden. "I place my bottle lamp upon thy *pé*, oh, *mystère* of dark and magical powers, a black bottle composed of *pimentchien* and Guinea-pepper and powdered lizard; of castor oil and precipitate and powder from a decomposed corpse."

I could not believe what I was hearing,

even as I found myself wondering whose corpse she referred to. Had she gone to the tomb behind the old sugar house in some macabre quest for the ingredient she had needed to compose her evil black bottle which was intended in some dark magical way to drive me away from Blackhurst Hall? Or was it meant to destroy me?

Suddenly I found myself running, the droning sound of her chilling Voodoo cabal following after me like a haunting death dirge, "*Poussez aller. Poussez aller,* Tracey O'Toole."

Mad, I thought. *Mad.* Did Valmir know? Did the others? Seena and Magda and Gabe? Did that explain the air of mystery which seemed to unite them in a conspiracy which I sensed was directed against me? Were they striving to maintain an illusion of sanity in the face of madness?

I ran faster, coming abreast of the thick wall of vines that climbed to hide the west wing gallery. I hesitated to catch my breath, pushing back flying strands of hair pulled free from my headband by the clutching shrubbery.

It was then that I saw a light, the only break in the black shadows behind the latticework of vines above me. It was scarcely more than a thread, shining along the edge of the French windows from behind heavy curtains.

In the next instant, I caught a movement on the gallery above me as someone moved from behind one of the thick columns and went toward the thin thread of light.

I stayed in the shadows watching, catching the quick flash of a white-trousered leg as whoever was there passed through a mottled pool of moonlight. Valmir.

He paused before the darkened French windows, his dark form blotting out the betraying slice of light that edged the tightly drawn portieres. I heard him tap lightly on the panes. When there was no response, he thrust the windows inward and stepped between them, pushing them swiftly closed behind him.

Chapter EIGHTEEN

I ran on. I wanted only to be away from that secretive part of the old house, away from the seething undercurrents of madness and mystery and the endless, terrifying questions that raced through my head.

I went past the rear of the house onto the path that would lead me across the narrow, lily-choked pool in the direction of the old kitchen and the overseer's office. The thought was in the back of my mind to go to the vault behind the old sugar house. But I would need a light. I thought then of the lamp I had seen standing on top of my grandfather's rolltop desk, and taking the path to the right, I went onto the office gallery, waiting behind the vines to make certain that I had not been followed.

The gardens appeared to be empty, filled with the soft, secretive sounds of night.

I tried the door. It opened easily beneath my touch and I went quickly to the desk, finding the lamp still standing where I had seen it. There were matches tucked beneath one of the pair of stags. Dropping them into the pocket of my robe, I went with the lamp toward the pale rectangle of moonlight which shone in through the open door.

Startled by a whisper of sound somewhere behind me, I spun around, half-expecting to find Gabe watching me from the dark stairwell as he had done that first time I had come here. But there was nothing. No one. I realized then that what I had heard had been the soft touch of a branch against one of the tall windows as a light breeze stirred around me.

Going then with my lamp, I started up the path which would lead me in the direction of the dovecotes and pigeonhouses and the old slave hospital which stood next to the "quarters."

The garden here was filled with lush, semi-tropical growth. Had it not been for the quickly rising moon, I should not have found my way so easily. I passed numerous small buildings half-buried in vines, among them an ancient spring house and a small, private chapel.

The sounds from the swamps had grown louder, and I became aware of wet grasses and reeds, attesting to the vast network of drainage ditches which had been dug to sweeten the surrounding marshes; ditches that had long since joined with the slimy, black fingers of the swamp to reclaim the low-lying areas of the overworked cane fields.

All of this I knew from my mother, aware that danger lurked in the outlying marshlands in the form of the deadly quagmires she had been taught to dread as a child. There had always been an air of malevolence surrounding the house, I thought, beginning with the superstitious slave stories of a treacherous, black quagmire known as The Devil's Well, hidden somewhere in the depths of the marshes like some dread Charybdis waiting to claim its unsuspecting victims.

The path I followed took a bend to the left, joining with a narrow road to pass through the old family orchard, the gnarled trees already beginning to bend beneath the weight of plums, peaches, and pears, and the lush purple figs my mother had relished as a child. I could see the rear of the two-story slave cabins between the knotted limbs, the windowless, brick walls rising to form a solid bulwark topped by the crumbling remains of tabby chimneys. There had been no cat 'n clay chimneys at Blackhurst, my mother had once told me.

The flimsy mud, clay and stick structures caught fire too easily, and Charles Blackhurst would not risk the lives of his valuable chattels by housing them in makeshift dwellings as had some of the neighboring planters.

The old sugar house loomed ahead at my left, its crumbling walls and broken stacks rising above the black line of the swamp, while on my right lay the billowing cane fields.

A faint trail, scarcely more than a snaking gray shadow in the midst of tangled mayhaw and blackberry vines, led away from the dusty road into the dark shadows beside the ancient sugar house, going in the direction of the Indian shell mound that had served as the Blackhurst burial ground for well over a century. I followed the dimly marked track, cradling the lamp with its fragile chimney in one arm while I reached with my free hand to lift the hem of my robe away from the thickly barbed vines.

Tall reeds and grasses traced the passage of an abandoned drainage ditch at the rear of the sugar house. The frogs croaking in the midst of the matted water hyacinths choking the narrow waterway fell silent at my approach, and I heard the wet splat of a turtle diving into shallow depths as I stepped onto a mossy footbridge.

There, only a few feet in front of me was the clamshell cemetery, the moonlight filtering down through moss-hung trees to cast strange shapes in the midst of the plastered-brick tombs. Charles Blackhurst, as had the French Acadians who came to this part of Louisiana during the latter half of the eighteenth century, discovered that because of the high water table, it was impossible to bury his dead in the ground. The new settlers had simply dug their graves and built their tombs in the huge heaps of discarded shells left behind by the Indians who had preceded them.

It was not difficult, even in that uncertain light, for me to find the original vault where, my mother had told me, that first bride named Amber was laid to rest. Much larger than its neighbors, the raised and pedimented tomb bore four stone heads at its upper corners, above a cornice of leafy anthemions darkly encrusted with lichens.

I didn't know what I had come here expecting to find. I was still too stunned by what I had just heard and seen to think clearly. Perhaps Valerie was mad, as I had begun to suspect. I kept hearing her low voice intoning her wild Voodoo chant.

Poussez aller. Poussez aller. Hurry and go. Hurry and go.

More chilling still, had that part of Valerie's macabre incantation which referred to the powder from a decomposed corpse any real basis in fact?

Dread made my hands damp as I moved slowly among the tombs, and the tangled vines that had taken root in the layers of decomposing humus covering the clamshell mound snatched at the toes of my slippers.

Ferns fringed the openings left for the caskets in the plastered-brick tombs, the feathery fronds growing out of the sealed crevices. I made out the lichen-etched pattern of the poppies of sleep carved into the marble face of the high-arched vault beside me. Below them was a worn inscription: *Beau Blackhurst.* The name meant nothing to me.

A row of vaults at one side of the old burial mound appeared to be newer than the rest and I went to them, searching for my cousin Rhea's name on the markers. But although I examined each of them carefully, tracing the carved plaques with my fingers to make certain that I had read them correctly, there was none engraved with Rhea Verret's name.

Only then did I turn toward the tomb Charles Blackhurst had erected to serve as a resting place for himself and the members of his immediate family. Because families had been immense then, often numbering into the dozens, the tomb was spacious.

Then, before my courage could desert me, I was sliding between the vault's heavy iron doors, their rusted hinges screeching loudly in protest as I forced my slight weight between them, taking care not to crack the fragile globe of my lamp against their ornate iron grilles.

There were perhaps a dozen crypts arranged at either side of the deep, narrow tomb. Its brick-paved floor had, through the years, become deeply layered with moss, which muffled my footsteps like deeply piled broadloom. The narrow, central passageway yawned before me like a cavern, the shadows cast by the flickering flame from my lamp deepening at its far end where it branched to form a T. Though I could not see beyond the rows of marble-sealed crypts, I guessed that the dark niches at either side of the tomb had been left free to serve as a storage space for tools and the vases and urns which would no doubt serve to decorate the numerous vaults on Memorial Day.

Silently I made my way toward the rear of the vault, reading the names carved into the plaques set into the sealed openings behind which the caskets rested. Freshly applied mortar shone gray-white around the edges of a plain, unmarked plaque. Here then was where my grandfather's remains had been put to rest, I thought, moving to the next of the sealed openings which, as I had expected, bore a marker inscribed with my grandmother's name and the dates of her birth and death. There were other markers engraved with the names of long-dead Blackhursts whose names I did not recognize, and farther back, near the rear of the tomb, yet another of the unmarked crypts, its plain seal seated loosely in the opening for the coffin, with no mortar securing it. I would need only to pull free the rectangular piece of stone in order to see what lay behind it, I thought with an involuntary little shiver. Assuming then that the crypt was reserved for some member of the family who was not yet deceased, Seena perhaps, or even Valmir, I went quickly to examine the next marker. *Vester Verret.* My Cajun uncle's name carved into the thickly veined marble seemed to prove me right, and I moved swiftly into the depths of the vault. But if I had expected to find my cousin Rhea's name engraved on the adjoining marker, I was disappointed. *Jonathan Bennett Blackhurst,* the ornately carved plaque said.

I turned then to examine the crypts on the far side of the dank passageway, thinking that it was possible that a marker had not yet been obtained to identify my cousin's remains, just as there was as yet no plaque to show where my grandfather was buried.

Ambre Aurore Lestant Blackhurst. The name leapt at me from a pale marble slab decorated with the sculptured image of a serpent swallowing its tail. The symbol of eternity . . . It was a moment or two before I realized that the flat stone seal which hid the opening for the coffin had been cleansed of the moist, dark mildew which grew profusely inside the tomb, scrolling the veined marble plaques with an intricate fretwork of dark patterns and tracings. Raising my lamp close to the carved stone, I peered at the dates inscribed beneath Amber's name inside the circle formed by the sinuously twining serpent, noticing for the first time a small, carved butterfly, its wings flaring out from its segmented body like delicately scalloped flower petals.

It was a moment or two before I recognized the small symbol for what it was: Psyche the butterfly, personification of the soul made immortal by Jupiter. I could not help wondering then what had possessed Charles Blackhurst to decorate his dead bride's grave with such a profusion of symbolism taken from ancient mythology. Had he imagined when he ordered that the small butterfly symbol be emblazoned inside the coil of the tail-swallowing serpent of eternal life that the mystic symbols might in some magical way bring Amber's spirit back to him? Or was it because of the obeah curse uttered by the dying slave dooming Amber's spirit to haunt Blackhurst Hall and its occupants forever that my ancestor had felt compelled to decorate her crypt in such a superfluous manner? Why not the poppies of sleep to give her eternal rest, I thought then with a cold little shudder, more deeply affected by the morbid trend my imagination had taken than I wanted to be.

Suddenly it seemed as though I were enveloped by some sinister spell which I could not shake free of and, lowering my lamp to light the floor ahead of me, I turned toward the tomb's low, arched doorway. In that same instant, I was arrested by a pale flash at the base of the marble slab which concealed Amber's casket. Raising my light again, I held the restlessly moving flame close to the dark seam at the base of the seal, noticing with a start that someone had recently chipped away a small portion of the darkly veined marble.

There were other pale marks etched into the marble and I realized then that someone had attempted to pry free the ancient seal. I had been vaguely aware of a rough texture beneath the soles of my slippers. Now I realized that what I had imagined before to be merely the shards of a broken brick scattered across the damp and mildewed paving, was in actuality broken pieces of mortar.

Lifting my lamp, I guided the glow from its wavering flame along the outer edges of the seal, a cold sense of shock going through me when I saw that not only had someone attempted to pry the marble slab from the casket opening, whoever it was had first removed the plaster from around its edges. I raised cautious fingers to touch the ancient stone, feeling it give slightly beneath my touch. I needed only to lift it free to have access to the coffin in which Amber had been buried. I remembered

Valerie's macabre incantation in which she had detailed the contents of her magic black bottle.

It seemed then that I could not escape quickly enough from the ancient vault, and I turned abruptly away from the broken crypt whose loosened seal threatened to come crashing down on my toes at any moment.

The fluttering glow from my lamp cast a myriad frightening shadows around me as I half-ran, half-stumbled toward the front of the vault. I was within a few feet of the half-open doorway when I heard a faint whisper of sound in the darkness behind me. My first thought was that my light touch had caused the marble seal set precariously into the front of Amber's crypt to settle. Then the sound repeated itself, clearer this time, so that I imagined for a paralyzing instant that it had been a footstep falling onto a loosened brick.

But how could that be? I was alone inside the vault. Holding my lamp firmly in both hands so that its shallow edge of light fell directly ahead of me, I turned slowly about.

A pale shape stood at the back of the tomb, half-hidden from me behind the black shadows which seemed to hover with a life of their own beyond the long rows of crypts. I imagined at first that my mind was playing tricks on me, that I only seemed to see someone there because of the morbid trend my thoughts had taken.

Then she moved, advancing a step or two toward me.

Amber. She wore the same bridal white she had worn when I had looked up to find her hovering beyond the stair's spiraling banister the night someone had waited for me near the second-floor landing, to fling a dark cloth over my head and put me inside the treacherous elevator cage.

"Who are you?" I had to know, I thought numbly. If not Valerie, who? Who at Blackhurst Hall wanted to destroy me?

I took a tentative step toward her, willing myself to be brave as I lifted my lamp in an effort to see her face more clearly. The veil she had worn when I had glimpsed her from inside the elevator fell now to cover her hollow features so that only her eyes were visible, glittering madly from behind its fragile folds.

"Go away!" she hissed in her queer, whispering voice. "Go away!" Her arms flew up in a nervously defensive gesture warning me not to come any nearer.

It was then that I saw on a growing wave

of horror that her right hand was missing. In its place was only a stump, the scarred flesh at its base showing pink through the misty white of her veil.

I screamed and spun around. I must have moved too quickly. For in that same moment, the globe from my lamp went flying, smashing with a loud, tinkling crash onto the bricks at my feet. The flame in my hand spiraled wildly in the swift wash of air caused by my panicky flight. Then, just as quickly, it flickered out, and I was wrapped in darkness.

Chapter NINETEEN

I ran toward the narrow rectangle of moon-light that shone beyond the door to the tomb. Forcing my way between the half-closed panels, I continued to run, the black-berry vines and twining tendrils of scupper-nong snatching at my flying feet as I ca-reened wildly between the high, arched vaults.

I should have taken heed from the grasp-ing vines which clutched about my ankles with needle-sharp barbs. But my only thought was to escape from the horribly maimed ghost woman who had confronted me from out of the black shadows at the rear of the tomb. *Amber.* Driven by an icy terror which was partly dread of the thing I had seen inside the vault, partly fear for my own sanity which I no longer trusted, I could give no thought then to caution.

I had gone only a few yards farther when there was a sharp, jarring tug on my foot and I went flying headlong against a stone urn looming suddenly before me at the base of one of the roughly plastered tombs.

I felt the tottering ornament sway beneath the impact of my head, even as I went crashing down, and the whole world was blotted out.

I fought my way up out of a strangling darkness, vaguely aware that someone clawed at my throat with fingers like icy spears.

I tried to scream. But no sound came. Then I realized that the fingers were my own, fighting to tear off the strangling strand of amber beads which belonged to neither me nor my mother.

I remembered then. There had been someone waiting for me when I returned home from the branch library where I had gone to look up the lines from Fuller's *Life of Monica* that my mother had quoted to me in her letter. I had heard his creaking footstep on the stair, heard the faint, terrifying sound of his breathing. He had come at me then, lunging . . . Turning to run, I caught my toe in the frayed runner and I flew downward, striking my head against the wall beside the stair. He had carried me upward then to my room, and I screamed for someone to come and rescue me from his insane assault. *Guy. Guy Lannin.* Where was he now?

I felt the knot at my neck, tearing frantically at the tiny, slick knobs of the tangled beads in an effort to free my windpipe. *Guy. Where was he?*

I opened my eyes. A monstrous moon was visible between gently swaying banners of moss, its pearly rays playing softly across my face. I lay in the midst of moist grasses and prickly vines beside a dark, humped shape which seemed somehow ominous.

Then suddenly there was the dark form of a man bending over me.

"Tracey!" Strong hands jerked me roughly upright, their agile fingers ripping fiercely at the choking beads, flinging them wildly aside.

Gabe. I stared desperately into his face, gulping in air in great, sobbing gasps.

"Tracey, are you all right?" I saw the savage gleam of his teeth against the tawny darkness of his face.

Mrs. Costain's description of the man she had seen lurking near my letter box in San Francisco flashed into my mind: *He looked like a foreigner of some kind to me, with his tanned skin and black eyes. His hair was black, too; as black as the Devil's own.* Was Gabe Guirlande the man she had seen? Did that explain how he knew that

278

the amber beads were a Blackhurst family heirloom and why they had been twisted around my neck again tonight?

"It was you!" I cried hysterically and felt him shaking me, his palm cracking sharply against my cheek.

"Stop that," he said. "Stop it at once and tell me what happened. Who did this to you? Answer me, Tracey. It's important."

"Why? Because you know I can identify you?"

"Because I am trying to save your life, for God's sake!"

"Amber," I said then in a small, disbelieving voice. "It was Amber. I saw her. There inside the vault."

He breathed an oath, pulling me roughly against him. I felt his mouth searching, finding my own. In that spellbinding moment I knew that, for all of his dark, threatening looks and regardless of Magda, he was as violently attracted to me as I was to him.

Then abruptly the spell between us was broken by the sharp, hissing crack of a whip.

We drew apart and I saw Magda silhouetted in pale moonlight, the blacksnake which was never far from her trailing like a venomous serpent from her hand.

The rest of what happened then faded into a blur. Vaguely I remember Gabe lifting me into his arms to carry me to the house, with Magda leading the way, her whip snapping out from time to time to slice clumps of grass and brambles from our path.

This time Gabe did not call Dr. Whitaker to drive out from town and examine the bruises on my neck and throat. It would mean answering questions, I thought as he bent over me to probe my abused flesh with fingers that were surprisingly gentle, questions he would prefer no one asked.

Assisted by a grim-faced Odalie, he smoothed some pungently soothing ointment onto the places where the beads had bitten cruelly into my skin.

"It's my own plaster salve, Miss Tracey," Odalie reassured me when I flinched away from his touch. "My own mama taught me how to make it before she died. No need for you to worry none. The ache and soreness will be gone out of your neck by mornin'."

Oddly enough the sharply astringent salve seemed already to have a reviving effect on me, its acrid fumes penetrating through my nostrils to clear my head.

"Odalie's the best conjure woman around," Gabe remarked.

I thought of Valerie perched high in the old live oak reciting her weird chant to her magic lamp.

Something of the doubt and distaste I felt must have shown in my face, for Gabe said, "If you're imagining this salve is comprised of some obscene ingredients, I assure you it's not. I've watched Odalie prepare it myself as a matter of scientific interest. It does wonders for the field hands when they come to me with their cuts and calluses."

"What's in it?" I dared then to ask.

"Just some goose eggs is all, child," Odalie said, tearing strips of soft, white cloth from what appeared to be a worn-out sheet. "A little unsalted hog's grease and some special powders I purchased from the old conjure woman who sells roots down by the swamp."

Powders. I fought down a wave of dizziness and nausea, wondering if it were possible that Valerie had obtained the ingredients for her magic lamp from the same conjure woman Odalie had mentioned. Or had my worst suspicions been confirmed when I discovered that Amber's crypt had recently been opened? Who was the ghostly apparition in the depths of the tomb? Was it Amber's spirit I had seen, intent on seeking revenge on whoever had dared to open her grave to desecrate her remains for the sake of some obscene obeah ritual? But there was no such thing as ghosts, I reminded myself, even as I remembered with a sudden, cold shudder that the ghost woman's right hand had been missing.

"There's terebinthine in it, as you've probably guessed from the smell of it, and a little vinegar-soaked verdigris," Gabe was saying. "For whatever good it may do, it can do you no harm."

"I've got you an infusion brewing, Miss Tracey," Odalie said. "It'll help draw the soreness out from the inside, if you swallow it like I tell you. That Miss Magda is gettin' mighty careless with that ugly old blacksnake she carries to do a thing like this to her own kin." The elderly black woman paused to click her tongue disapprovingly.

"But it wasn't . . ." I started to say.

Then I saw the fierceness in Gabe's eyes and fell silent.

"Knowin' Miss Magda, you're lucky she didn't take your head clean off." Odalie

282

bent over me to wind a soft length of clean cloth around my neck. "Same way she takes the heads off chickens do I need me a fresh pullet for the *Gombo Zhébes* she's always callin' on me to fix for her. I tell her the recipe calls for salt meat. But nothing will have it but I fix it with chicken just so she can find an excuse to kill the chickens the hands have scratchin' for their own use down behind the quarters. Miss Magda say that's how she keeps in practice. 'In practice for what?' I asked her. But she don't have no answer for me."

I listened disbelievingly, thinking that my father had been right about my cousins when he had referred to them as a quartet of savages, wondering again if Rhea had been like the others, fierce, sullen. *Cajun.* Like Gabe Guirlande.

Valmir alone among those who lived in the old house appeared to be in some degree civilized. Seena was also an exception. I was beginning to realize that she was oddly intimidated by her offspring. She seemed almost frightened of them at times, as though they had gained some strong hold over her which she was powerless to break.

As for Valmir, I could not help feeling wary of him, for all of his easy, gentleman-planter's charm. As close as he and Valerie were, he must know that his twin was involved in the practice of obeah magic directed at me, in an effort to hasten my departure from Blackhurst. And what of Valmir's stealthy visit to the mansion's west wing? I could not so easily forget that I had seen him glide secretly from behind one of the tapered, Tuscan pillars to tap expectantly on the French windows, windows from behind which a whispering voice claiming to be Amber's had warned me to go away.

Yet he alone among those who lived at Blackhurst had seemed at all pleased to see me upon my arrival here. *If you want me for anything — anything at all — just call my name and I'll come running,* he had told me that first morning at breakfast. Did that explain why Valerie felt compelled to direct her witch's power at me through the medium of her black bottle? Because of her jealous attitude toward Valmir, who had not hesitated to show his appreciation of me in a flirtatious way?

I did not doubt for an instant that Valerie viewed me as a threat to her clannish relationship with her twin brother, in spite of the fact that I was their cousin. While Magda was equally determined not to allow my presence to interfere in any way with her relationship with Gabe Guirlande. She had made it clear to me from the start that she considered Gabe her own personal property and that anything I might do to jeopardize her claim would be nothing short of foolhardy. The vicious snap of her whip which had served to separate us when she had found him kissing me in the old cemetery had told me that as plainly as if she had shouted a warning into my ear.

And what of Gabe? As stunned as I had been from the fall I had taken, I had sensed during that spellbound moment when our mouths found each other that I was the one he wanted. But in what way? There were dark forces in him that I could not fathom. I had never been drawn to a man before in just this way, and it was not clear in my mind what he expected from me, nor what I expected from him.

I was a fool to trust any one of them, I thought, as I glanced up after Odalie had finished dressing my bruises, and found Gabe watching me. His black eyes seemed suddenly more knowledgeable than I wanted them to be.

"I'll go fetch your tea now," Odalie said, leaving me alone with him.

"Feeling better?" he asked.

I managed a little nod. "Much. I'll be fine after I've rested." I paused. "Why did you tell Odalie Magda did this to me with her whip? I told you what happened."

"You were rambling," he said.

"But I saw someone . . . something inside the old vault," I insisted.

"We'll talk about it tomorrow," he said, laying a flat palm on my forehead. "In the meantime, I want you to drink Odalie's infusion like a good girl. Her feelings will be hurt if you refuse it."

"I suppose you know the recipe, or receipt, as Odalie would say," I said with a touch of sarcasm.

He nodded. "And the ingredients are innocent, if that's what's bothering you. Saint-John's-wort. Some wild cresses. The old woman she told you about digs the roots along some hidden branch. Branch as in brook or creek, not tree limb," he added with a touch of humor.

"And that's all?" I asked suspiciously.

"Give or take an herb or two," he said. "There's some sprigs of scurvy grass in it and a few slices of fresh citron are added to make it more palatable. In the old days, the brew was thought to be more efficacious if it contained a sizable lump of purified saltpeter. It was used to medicate sick slaves when they came down with yaws or scurvy, and I suppose the saltpeter served to take the fight out of the more lively bucks, as they called them. Odalie has civilized it by replacing the saltpeter with a few dollops of raw honey from the hives down behind the old sugar house. It's really quite tasty."

"It sounds awful," I said.

"Surely you can choke it down just to keep Odalie happy."

"Did she give it to my grandfather when he was ill?" I asked.

"He had great faith in all of Odalie's home remedies."

"But they didn't save his life," I said.

"You know, don't you, that I'd give anything if they had." Gabe's expression darkened. "He was one of the finest men I've ever known. He influenced me greatly. That's one of the reasons I felt it only right for me to move out here to help run the plantation now he's gone. It's the way he'd have wanted it." He paused, eyeing me quizzically. "Incidentally, there's something I've been meaning to speak to you about. Now seems as good a time as any, especially after what happened tonight. I can imagine you must be anxious now to leave . . ."

"But I'm not," I said quickly. "Not until I've succeeded in finding my mother."

He held up a slim hand. "Hear me out," he said. "What I was about to suggest is that you sell to me any claim you feel you might have to your grandfather's estate. I've arrived at what I consider to be a fair price for anything he may have seen fit to leave you in his will. There's no way, of course, that we can know just what his last testament consists of. But I won't cheat you if I can help it." He named what sounded to me like a ridiculously low sum if it should happen, as he seemed to imagine was possible, that my grandfather had included me among his heirs.

"But why?" I blurted. "Especially when you've no guarantee that he left me anything at all. In fact, that is the last thing I expect to have happen."

"I have my reasons," he said.

I watched him curiously, as if I could read his intentions in his face. But whatever motive had prompted his strange offer was hidden from me.

I said, "You must know that I had never even met my grandfather. My mother left here before I was born. Besides, it's an old family tradition for the plantation to go to the *male* heir next in line to inherit.

Knowing the kind of man my grandfather was, I doubt that it would even have occurred to him to change it. In which case, everything will go to Valmir."

"Valmir is a Verret," Gabe stated.

"He's the only male heir my grandfather had," I said.

He looked at me quietly, his stolid, Cajun silence somehow intense and, I could not help thinking, dangerous.

"Am I to take it then that you're refusing my offer?" he finally said.

"How can I accept an offer for something that doesn't belong to me?" I countered.

Again he hesitated, his dark gaze burning into me. When at last he spoke, his voice was grim. "You're making a mistake, you know. A terrible mistake. I only hope you don't live to regret it."

Chapter TWENTY

I slept soundly. There were no bad dreams, no stealthy noises to disturb me. Or if there were, I slept peacefully through them, drugged, I suspected, by the hot conjure tea Odalie had brought me.

My watch, which I had laid on the bedside table, told me when I woke that it was nearly nine. The others would have breakfasted by now and have gone their separate ways. I decided that I would take a leisurely bath in the big old tub in the hope that it would help clear my mind so that I could reach a sensible decision about where next to turn in my search for my mother.

My decision made, I sat up abruptly in bed, flinging my legs across the edge of the mattress to slide bare feet into waiting slippers. Unwrapping the soft dressings Odalie had wound around my neck the previous night to prevent her pungent salve from soiling the bedclothes, I realized that the old woman had been right. The soreness where the beads had bruised my throat had all but vanished. Looking back on the series of events which had overtaken me in the old cemetery, I found myself wondering if any of it could possibly have been real. Had I only imagined that I saw a ghost woman whose right hand was missing watching me from out of the depths of the Blackhurst tomb? Had the tangled strand knotted around my neck when I regained consciousness following the spill I had taken been nothing more than a gnarled length of vine?

Going to the ancient armoire, I reached for the discarded candy box where I had hidden the beads. The box was empty. I thought then that there had been ample opportunity for any one of those who lived in the house to slip into my room during my absence to take the beads. The hiding place I had found for them had not been nearly so ingenious as I had wanted to believe. My next thought was that of all those who lived in the house, Gabe Guirlande alone had known that I had the amber necklace in my possession. Was it something more than a coincidence that it had been Gabe I found bending over me in the old cemetery when my senses had begun to clear? Suppose it were Gabe who wanted to be rid of me. Suppose he were the one who was responsible for my mother's mysterious disappearance as well. How could I force his hand? Who could I turn to for help?

I went to the French windows, throwing open the velvet portieres to let in the daylight, as though by doing so, I could view my dilemma more clearly. The soles of my slippers grated onto what I imagined at first to be sand sprinkled across the polished cypress floorboards directly beneath the low sill. Puzzled when I tried to imagine how the coarse grains came to be there, I stooped to examine them more closely. I discovered that it was not sand at all but a queer, mottled mixture of finely ground shells and moldy leaf loam. Small pieces of freshly torn leaves shone in the midst of the coarsely granulated rubble. Picking up one of the shredded bits of vegetation, I discovered that it had come from an elm tree.

I was still on my knees staring in puzzled bewilderment at the strange mixture in my hand when a light tap sounded on my door.

"You awake yet, Miss Tracey?" Odalie's voice called softly.

Before I could brush my fingers clean, the door inched open to admit her grizzled head poking in above the steaming tray she carried.

"What you doin' down there like that, child?" the old woman admonished me, going to put the tray on the table beside the settee. She came then to peer curiously at my soiled fingers. "Do you know what that is, Miss Tracey?" she said in surprise.

I looked again at the dirt scattered haphazardly across the floorboards in front of me. There had been moldy humus blanketing the shell mound where the Blackhurst graves were, I thought, thinking too that it was possible that Gabe, or perhaps even Magda, had tracked in some of the finely ground soil when Gabe carried me back to my room. But in this quantity? From the look of it, someone had flung several handfuls of the loose dirt through my open windows while I slept.

More bewildered than ever, I looked up into Odalie's startled black face.

"Who did this, child?" Odalie asked then. "Who throwed conjure dirt through your window while you asleep? First Miss Magda wraps her whip around your throat and like to behead you. Then I find you here like this, your floor all covered with dirt from underneath the old obeah tree."

I thought of Valerie.

I said, "What does it mean?"

"It means somebody wants you out of this house mighty bad," Odalie said, going to get the hearth broom, which leaned against the marble face of the fireplace and attacking the dirt furiously. She swept it onto a magazine that had been lying on my bedside stand and threw it into the bushes below the gallery. "Bad enough to go to the graveyard in the middle of the night to gather up seven handfuls of dirt from underneath the old obeah tree to throw at your window," she continued. "See the little hunks of leaves there on the rug? No mistaking them. That's elm. It takes a lash made from the stalk of a bayahonde to make the magic work, but any old whip will do in a pinch."

I did not need to ask her whom she suspected. But she was wrong, I thought, just as she had been wrong about the bruise marks on my neck. They had not come from the pellets knotted into the tail of Magda's blacksnake, as Odalie had been led to believe, by Gabe no doubt. Nor was it Magda who had thrown the dirt from beneath the old obeah tree through my window, I thought. More likely, it was Valerie.

I said with a great deal more aplomb than I felt, "Luckily for me, I don't believe in such nonsense."

Odalie gave me a frightened look. "Hush, child. Don't let Manman Brigitte hear you say that. Your fate is in her hands now. No need for whoever put this hex on you to hang around."

"Who in heaven's name is Manman Brigitte?" I demanded, growing suddenly impatient with her veiled implication that some power outside myself had invaded my room merely as a result of a few handfuls of cemetery dirt.

"The most ancient of the dead," Odalie said in a hushed voice. "She's the wife of Baron Samedi, lord of the cemetery. That's where she live. There in the trees and the shell piles and the old vaults. But the elm is her favorite haunt. Those who want favors from her sprinkle its roots with raw clairin and wheat flour and peanuts and cornmeal. Those are the things she likes best. Manman Brigitte hears you then, most especially if you strikes out at her tree with a lash."

Were there actually people who still believed in the ancient Voodoo practices such as Odalie described? Valerie? But how could she? How could anyone?

I said in a small, disbelieving voice, "You think it was Magda who threw that dirt at my window, don't you."

"I've got no use for Miss Magda's high-handed ways," Odalie grumbled, going to the low table to remove the silver covers from the plates of food she had brought me. "Masta Benjamin felt the same way, I reckon. More than once I heard him complain about those young uns of Miss Seena's. He swore he'd leave them all paupers if they didn't mend their ways. Miss Magda. And that Masta Valmir and Miss Valerie, always slippin' away into the swamps to look for Lafitte's lost gold. And that poor Miss Rhea . . ." She fell suddenly silent, as though, I thought, she had only just remembered that Rhea was dead.

I sat down at the low table, taking a sip of the rich, black coffee Odalie poured for me.

When I had swallowed the scalding brew, I said, "I don't suppose there's any real chance that my cousins might find the gold they're after."

Odalie made a low, snorting noise. "Some *couzan* Cajun they know claims he seen that pirate Lafitte's longboat stickin' up out of the mud. Claims he seen the prow as plain as day. Masta Valmir, he believes that wild tale because he wants to. He and Miss Valerie been on the trail of that lost gold ever since they were knee-high, same as their pappy before them."

"Ves Verret?" I said.

"Him," Odalie said, reverting unconsciously to the Cajun patois I had heard her use before. "He didn't talk nor spit nor sweat nor curse while he was diggin'. But it didn't help him none. He never found so much as a dime's worth of gold in all the years he spent grubbin' in the mud like the catfishes and turtles. He was like my old grandpappy's wagon, always rattled the loudest when it was comin' away from the sugar house."

"But it's true that Lafitte cruised and pillaged throughout all of the bayou country," I said.

"That sounds like something Masta Valmir would say," Odalie commented. "Most likely if Lafitte did bury his gold here on Blackhurst land like some say, it's at the bottom of the Devil's Well by now. Ain't nobody ever find it there."

"Then there really is such a place," I said.

"Hearsay, like the stories about Lafitte and his gold," Odalie said shortly. "There are some that say Lafitte himself is buried right here on Blackhurst land and others who claim he didn't come this way at all;

that he's buried over on Bayou des Oies. It's the same with his gold and the Devil's Well, I reckon. Maybe they is and maybe they ain't. Same as the servants who work in this house," Odalie added, giving me a shuttered look.

"I don't understand," I said.

"Servants in this house got to see and don't see, hear and don't hear," the old black woman said. "Be a good idea if you was to do the same, I reckon."

Chapter TWENTY-ONE

But if Odalie could close her eyes and ears to the strange happenings inside the old house, I could not. Without her strong conjure tea to lull me, I did not sleep that night. I did not even try. Pulling on my robe, I went out onto the gallery where I stood behind the thickly laced vines and tried to think what I must do.

Something . . . someone was hiding in the sealed west wing, that much I was sure of. Someone whose right hand was missing. Whoever the ghost woman was, those who lived in this house did not want me to know about her. Even Odalie and her husband Henri saw and did not see, heard and did not hear, pretending an ignorance they did not have so that in essence, they became accomplices if only by default in the conspiracy against me.

My cousin Valmir for reasons I could not possibly guess, found it necessary under cover of night to slip in to visit whoever hid from me behind the west wing windows, attempting, I suspected, to elude even Valerie.

I must find my missing mother and leave this house as quickly as possible, I thought, attempting to sort my questing thoughts into some semblance of logical order. If I were to do that, I must continue to search the house for some clue that would tell me where she had gone. But first I must have a light, since it seemed imperative that I carry out my search undetected by the others. I could not go stumbling about the unfamiliar rooms in darkness, nor would it be wise for me to flick on switches as I went, since I wanted to keep my movements secret. There were too many eyes watching me. Above all, I was aware of the ghost woman's stealthy interest in me, the thought of that pale, mutilated form who seemed to appear when she was least expected sending a cold shiver through me.

I tried then to think where Seena might keep a flashlight that I could use without giving myself away. There were several islands of ancient furniture located along the length of both the second-story and ground-floor hallways. I had noticed a number of old sofas and console tables standing beneath the gilt-framed portraits of my ancestors, their brass-handled drawers filled, no doubt, with an accumulation of odds and ends. It seemed logical now for me to assume that I might find the flashlight I sought in one of the drawers, tucked out of sight in the midst of the usual household clutter.

I would start with the upstairs hallway, I decided with that same calm, cool logic, and if I failed to find a flashlight in one of the table drawers there, I would carry my search to the downstairs corridor.

Stepping across the low sill into my room, I went to the bedside table to glance at my watch. It was just midnight. The others would have retired to their rooms by now, leaving the way clear for me, I thought.

Nevertheless, I pressed my ear to the door panels to make certain no one stirred in the hallway outside before I turned the key in the lock and cautiously twisted the knob.

The hallway was dark save for a dim nightlight at its far end near the spiraling staircase. Going quickly to a Lannuier sofa table which stood opposite my door beneath a mirror, I pulled open the central drawer and rummaged swiftly through sheafs of old letters and ballpoint pens. When the drawer failed to yield what I sought, I went quickly to the far end of the hallway where it branched before double doors to penetrate the far-flung wings. The full moon lighted the rear courtyard beyond the gallery almost to the brightness of day, and shreds of light penetrated behind the thick vines to glitter faintly on the panes of the French doors. If anyone were watching past the edge of a louvered door behind me, they would see me standing in stark silhouette before the square panes, and I moved quickly into the shadows, going in the direction of the east wing, where a dark grouping of chairs and tables was vaguely visible.

Feeling my way past a large sofa, I crouched before a small table, my fingers fumbling blindly for the drawer pull. The first thing I found when I reached cautiously to explore the inside of the long, narrow drawer was the light I sought, the round, metal barrel sliding into my palm almost as though it had been waiting there for me.

Taking the flashlight from its hiding place, I had started to press the switch to make certain the batteries still worked, when from somewhere dangerously nearby came the soft click of a door latch. My first instinct was to hide, and, crouching low to the floor, I squeezed quickly into the narrow space between the spindle-legged table and the high curved arm of the sofa.

Resting my weight on my knuckles and knees, the flashlight clutched awkwardly in my curled fingers, I peered cautiously along the hallway in the direction of the west wing.

The faint rays of moonlight fell in pale silvery splotches onto the polished floorboards before the gallery doors, causing the hallway beyond to seem blackly cavernous and somehow threatening. I was certain the sound I had heard was from that direction and I continued to watch, alerted to catch the least hint of movement in that endless sea of darkness. I suppose that in the back of my mind was the thought that the ghost woman would somehow float eerily into my line of vision, her bridal white flowing behind her.

A pale rectangle of light shone briefly as whoever was there slid swiftly between the west wing doors.

But this time it was not the ghost woman I saw. In the split second before the doors closed behind him, I recognized Valmir.

There was the soft, sliding sound of metal as whoever was hiding behind those forbidden doors turned a key to slip the bolt back into place, and a moment later, I heard Valmir's hurrying footsteps as he came toward me, turning before the gallery doors to disappear along the long central corridor.

I had started to creep from my hiding place when again I heard the soft sound of a bolt gliding along its metal groove. Still watching, I glimpsed a pale form emerge from a darkened side-door a short distance past the branching turn. For a stunned moment or two, I imagined that this time it was the ghost woman who claimed to be Amber.

Then, as she crossed through pale splashes of moonlight, I saw that it was Valerie following on stealthy feet in Valmir's wake. I realized then that she had been there all along; that for reasons of her own, she had taken it upon herself to spy on her handsome brother. The plot around me seemed to thicken when it occurred to me that, perhaps like myself, Valerie did not know who was hiding in the mansion's west wing. I found myself wondering as I had done before if it could possibly be my mother.

I waited to make certain that the twins had gone before I tried my light. When I dared at last to press the switch forward along the metal barrel, the piercing spot startled me with its brightness. Crawling cautiously from my hiding place, I went slowly toward the locked doors, more curious than ever to know what lay behind them.

Reaching with trembling fingers, I tried the handles that secured them.

But it was no use. The tightly locked panels refused stubbornly to yield.

Remembering then that I had seen Valmir tap lightly on the French windows which overlooked the part of the gallery that fronted the west wing, I thought impulsively that I would do the same. If whoever was hiding there was in the habit of admitting Valmir when he gave his gently tapping signal, it was possible that it might work for me. My heart pounding with a wild excitement which was partly dread of what I might find were I to gain admittance to those forbidden rooms, partly fear for my own safety in the face of the madness I was certain lurked behind the west wing's locked doors and windows, I returned to my room.

Drawing aside the heavy portieres, I stepped swiftly out through the French windows onto the gallery. Pausing before the west wing windows where the pale form I had seen hovering behind the dark vines had vanished, I drew a deep breath to garner my courage. But before I could raise my fingers to tap on the glass as I had seen Valmir do, I was alerted by a pale movement at the far end of the gallery where it turned to circumvent the jutting main section of the house.

I imagined at first that it was some errant shifting of the moonlight that had caught my eye.

Then I saw her. She stood as she had done that other time, scarcely more than a pale shadow against the blackly latticed vines. Then as I watched her, she turned toward the corner of the gallery, pausing briefly before she vanished past the dark turn beyond the line of my vision.

I had the chilling sensation that she was luring me, drawing me after her toward danger. But it was as if she had acquired some strange dark power over me, and I could not stop myself from going after her.

Numbly I thought, even as I began to run through pale splashes of moonlight in the direction which she had taken: *This time she will not escape me. This time I will overtake her.*

Snapping on my light, I shot its bright beam past the corner after her. She whirled, the piercing spot briefly illuminating her eyes so that they shone with a fanatic light from out of their abysmal hollows. Then she darted forward once more, going away from me around a corner toward the rear of the house. Still I went after her, my light catching her in the split second before she vanished from my view behind the French doors which opened into the central hallway.

I felt suddenly drained, thinking that she had escaped from me once more to return to her lair behind the west wing's locked doors.

But I was wrong. When I stepped into the house a moment or two later, I saw her again, poised at the far end of the central corridor near the spiraling staircase. I knew then that she wanted me to follow her. Throwing all caution to the winds, I went after her as she whirled suddenly toward the stairs, her left hand reaching to glide smoothly along the curving banister as she plunged lightly downward.

Again I found her waiting, my light illuminating the pale oval of her face when I darted its bright beam into the central shaft past the old elevator cage, the wrought-iron grilles casting a dark pattern of garlanded leaves and flowers across the shimmering whiteness of her bridal gown.

She flitted along the ground-floor hallway toward the front of the house, her veil floating behind like a misty cloud. For a spellbinding instant, she stopped to peer through a darkened doorway, as though it had been her intention to enter there. When I reached the place where she had hesitated, I saw that the half-open door led into the library, the spot from my flashlight picking out ponderous dark tomes protected behind leaded-glass doors.

Hurrying on, I glimpsed her next in the garden, beyond the ghostly gray pillars of the veranda. And still I followed, a small corner of my mind reminded of the mad Ophelia, as the ghost woman flitted like a pale moth between moon-misted clumps of jessamine and parkisonia.

The beam from my light caught her as she turned onto the path which led past the old summer kitchen and the overseer's office, and I saw with a nightmare clarity that she wore the Blackhurst ambers, the small, honey-toned globules reflecting in that piercing light like drops of fire.

I think I knew then where she would take me, and yet I followed.

The night sounds of the swamps were all around me, rising insistently on the heavily scented air. Somewhere in the distance, an owl hooted, while nearer at hand there was only the soft fall of my running footsteps as I went after her along the dusty road which went in the direction of the old cemetery.

There was no sign of the ghost woman among the tombs, when I crossed the narrow footbridge behind the old sugar house going toward the ancient shell mound where my ancestors were buried.

Playing the beam from my flashlight wildly about, I scanned the dense shadows beneath the ancient live oaks, and the giant cypress beyond which the swamp began, my eyes straining to catch the glimmer of bridal white that would tell me where she had gone.

"Amber?" I called softly, a sense of dread coupled with a surge of disbelief going through me at the sound of my own voice calling the name of a girl who had been dead for well over a century.

Where was she? Why had she brought me here? I went slowly forward into the midst of the arched vaults, the smell of the nearby swamp rising dankly around me, as though it had reached to penetrate beneath the piled shells, its hidden black waters nourishing the riotously growing vines which crept over the darkly humped backs of the plastered tombs.

Suddenly, without knowing why, I felt drawn toward the huge family vault which dominated the center of the eerily shadowed mound. I was within a few feet of the darkly spreading elm which Odalie had called an obeah tree, when I was startled by a sudden loud clattering sound. It was a moment or two before I realized that the shattering noise had come to me from inside the old tomb.

My knees suddenly began to tremble when I recalled the loosened seal which had blocked the opening to the crypt where Amber was buried. Was that the sound I had heard? The marble slab someone had taken great pains to loosen by chipping away the sealing plaster — had it gone crashing onto the tomb's brick-paved floor? Was Amber inside, waiting even now for me to come to investigate the sudden echoing noise? Was this the way she had chosen to show me where she had gone?

I hesitated. In that same instant, she appeared before me, hovering briefly before the yawning black mouth of the old vault. Then just as quickly, she vanished, fluttering nervously away from me behind the spreading shadows of the obeah tree.

It seemed to me then that she was trying

to show me something inside the vault. Or did I only imagine that it was her intention for me to go inside the ancient tomb where my ancestors lay buried?

Directing the beam from my light past the ancient elm tree, I searched the black shadows beside the swamp for some sign which would tell me what she wanted. But if she had been there at all, she was gone.

Moving on shaking legs, I squeezed between the doors of the ancient vault, setting the sagging iron panels screeching on their rusted hinges. Somewhere nearby, a nightbird shrieked its alarm, the sound assaulting my shattered nerves so that it was all I could do to keep from crying out.

Swinging up my light, I pointed the beam into the darkness behind the rows of crypts. In that same instant, I saw on the brick pavement a blank seal that had concealed the coffin opening of one of the crypts I had assumed before was empty. The crashing sound it had made when it fell had been the sound I heard. I was relieved to discover that it had not been caused by the loosened marble plaque which hid Amber's coffin.

I started to turn away, driven by sudden dread, when the beam from my light picked out a pale shape inside the vacant crypt whose seal had fallen free. I moved nearer to the dank, black opening, shooting the beam from my light inside. Something white was bundled into the cavernous hole, and my first thought was that it was Amber, clad in her bridal gown and veil. But how was that possible when I had seen her only moments before, going in the direction of the swamp?

My fingers turned to ice as I reached forward to touch gingerly the tightly bundled cloth. Was this what the ghost woman had wanted to show me? What was inside the twisted length of heavy fabric which I saw now was a patterned brocade that must once have served to drape Blackhurst Hall's windows.

Gently I pried at a corner of the frayed fabric.

It was then that I saw it, a glistening lock of black hair very like my own, which had escaped from between the tightly wrapped layers of cloth. I must have started, for in the next instant, a fold of the worn cloth came free in my hand to reveal bloodless features staring in sightless panic at the mouth of the crypt.

The face I looked at belonged to my mother.

I must have cried out in grief and despair. For there was a sudden, faint scraping sound somewhere behind me and a hoarse voice whispered, "That's right, Tracey O'Toole. Your mother is dead, just as you will be."

I screamed. But before I could spin around, something wrapped itself around my neck, pulling me brutally off balance. In the split-second before my flashlight went flying, I glimpsed the dreadful row of blue bruises marking the pale flesh of my dead mother's throat.

I clawed at the slimy bricks beneath me in an effort to reach the legs of my attacker. But it was no use. The choking cord tightened around my neck, and I fought then to loosen the clammy string of beads which bit unmercifully into my flesh, strangling my breath in my throat.

As though from a great distance, I heard the sudden, sharp snap of a whip and a woman's voice hissing, "No! Not this way! Not here! Not now!"

Suddenly the pressure on my windpipe eased, and I was vaguely aware of a dark form moving past me into the depths of the tomb. Scrambling to my feet, I ran gasping out into the moonlit night, dodging wildly between the looming vaults in the direction of the narrow footbridge.

From out of the dark shadows beside the old sugar house came a man, his arms reaching to halt my headlong flight. I tried to veer away from him. But I was too late. His arms caught and held me.

"Gabe!" I gasped, a feverish reaction sweeping through me. "Gabe!"

I clung to him then, out of a desperate need for someone to console me.

"Tracey? What is it? What's happened?" He lifted me in his arms and carried me away from the black shadows of the old sugar house into a bright pool of moonlight. His dark eyes glittered above me, searching my upturned face for answers.

"Magda," I whispered. "And someone else . . ." I broke off, attempting to recall exactly what I had seen, what I had heard.

"Magda?" His voice lacked conviction.

He knows, I thought then. *He knows that Magda wants me dead, Magda and that other stealthily slinking being . . .* Who was it that had slid past me into the depths of the old tomb upon Magda's command, prompted by the deadly snap of her whip? Gabe? Was it possible that he had defied her to follow after me when I ran?

"Did you see who was with her?" His voice intruded into my numbed thoughts.

314

"No," I whispered quickly. "No."

Above me, his face was a mysterious blending of light and shadow in the glow from the moon. He stood me on my feet. But he kept his arms locked around me so that I could not move.

"You know, don't you?" I heard myself saying in that same small, stunned voice. "You know who it was that tried to kill me."

"Oh my God!" His voice was scarcely more than a fierce murmur.

I trembled as he bent to kiss me. His mouth found my own, the warmth from his body searing through me to drive out the icy numbness that had paralyzed me. Vaguely it occurred to me to tear myself free from him while there was still time.

But his grip was so strong that I could not have pulled away from him if I had wanted to.

Chapter TWENTY-TWO

Some self-protective instinct rose up in me so that, during the next few days, I was able to convince myself that it was not my mother I had seen lying dead in the family tomb, but my missing cousin, Rhea.

The result was that I became increasingly obsessed with thoughts of my cousin whom, Seena had told me, had met with some terrible accident. Had someone strangled her, using Amber's beads? Was that the "accident" Seena had referred to when she told me of the dreadful thing that had happened, something so terrible that she could not bring herself to tell me the details surrounding my cousin's death?

That evening, I went down early to dinner to find Odalie alone in the dining room, putting the finishing touches on the elaborately set table. A painting of a dark-haired young woman whose coloring was much like my own had replaced Amber's portrait above the mantel. I went to stare curiously into features which seemed somehow familiar, realizing that the portrait might have been a painting of my mother as a young girl.

Behind me, Odalie said, "That's your great-grandfather's old-maid sister. She could have married anybody she chose. But the only man she ever cared for was killed in the War, and she would look at no other man after that."

"What was her name?" I asked.

"Miss Rhea. Miss Rhea Lorainne."

Rhea. Rhea Lorainne. Dead, I thought. Dead in the old family vault.

I said in a small, dull voice, "She's very beautiful. I suppose my cousin Rhea looked a great deal like her."

"No. That Miss Rhea has reddish-colored hair, poor thing." Something in Odalie's voice alerted me.

"My cousin Rhea was homely then?" I turned curiously to face her.

"Not in the way you're thinkin', Miss Tracey." Odalie's face darkened, as if a blind had closed behind it.

"In what way then?" I persisted.

"She was thrown off her horse and dragged when she was barely out of her teens," Odalie said guardedly. "The rein caught around her wrist, and her hand was pulled clean off from her body."

"How awful!" I said in a stunned voice.

There was a slight movement beyond the doorway. I glanced over to see Magda looking in at us, her whip coiled loosely against her thigh.

"What's so awful?" my cousin demanded, her black eyes glinting suspiciously as she strode into the room.

"Rhea's accident," I said. "It must have been ghastly, having the same thing happen to her that had happened to Amber."

"I told you we're cursed," Magda said calmly. "Did Odalie tell you Rhea was wearing the Blackhurst ambers when it happened?"

I shook my head numbly.

"Well, she was. She was always fascinated with Amber's story, and, oddly enough, she resembled Blackhurst's first bride to a remarkable degree. The whole sad affair makes one wonder if there might not be something to the reincarnation theory after all." She gave me an arch look. "What about it, Tracey? Are you a believer? Or a skeptic like me?"

"A skeptic about what, darling?" Seena's voice said.

I realized she had entered the room without my seeing her, absorbed as I was in my own tumultuous emotions.

"Reincarnation, ghosts, that sort of thing." Magda shrugged indifferently.

"That's Valerie's forte," Seena commented, her tone disapproving.

Magda looked at me. "Perhaps you should ask Valerie about what happened to Rhea, then. Her observations could prove interesting."

Seena's face had turned suddenly chalky.

"Rhea?" she said in a small, trembling voice. "You haven't been discussing her, have you?" She looked accusingly at Magda.

"Tracey was curious about her is all," Magda said easily.

Seena flashed me a desperate look. "It was my fault, you know, that she died. I had asked her to ride out to the fields to do an errand for me. Insisted that she go." Seena's voice threatened to break. "She . . . died as a result of the amputation," she continued after awhile. "It was dreadful, her hand mangled, hanging by barely a thread . . . It happened shortly before your mother returned to Blackhurst Hall to attend your grandmother's funeral. Trouble always happens in three's, they say," my aunt added weakly.

Did she mean to imply that my mother's arrival had been the third disaster to overtake them? Had she hated my mother that desperately? Desperately enough to kill her when she had appeared here a second time to help nurse my ailing grandfather?

I felt suddenly ill and muttering an excuse, I fled from the room, ignoring the startled looks Valmir and Valerie gave me as I shot past them into the hall.

Later that night, unable to sleep, I stepped out onto the gallery. Already the moon had risen over the gardens below me, lighting the billowing cane fields beyond the swinging strands of moss to the brightness of day.

Someone moved along the dusty road in the direction of the old sugar house. Someone who wore white. I stepped swiftly back into my room, going with hurrying footsteps into the hall and down the spiraling staircase.

But this time it was not the ghost woman I followed. It was Valerie. Running along the moonlit road in an effort to catch her, I watched her vanish into the black shadows behind the old sugar house, going in the direction of the swamp.

I rounded a corner of the crumbling old building, catching the pale flash of the white blouse she wore in the midst of the palmettos that grew near the edge of the cane fields. Then once more she vanished, disappearing into the black shadows of the towering cypress trees that grew out of the swamp.

I went more slowly then, picking my way carefully between shimmering fingers of water, the thick scent of wild mallow rising around me. A huge cypress rose before me, dangling thick ropes of moss. I went past it, following a high rise of ground between clumps of wild cane that reached my shoulders.

Somewhere nearby, an alligator bellowed. There was a sudden, quick scuttling near my feet. A muskrat, I thought.

Still I pressed on, my senses numbed by a queer, dark power that compelled me.

I have no idea how long I trudged between treacherous stretches of murky water and rattling palmetto thickets before it occurred to me that I was lost. I went in circles then, attempting to trace my way back to the comparative safety of the mansion.

But it was no use. I dropped to the ground exhausted, pressing my fevered forehead to my upraised knees, holding my hands tightly against my ears to shut out the myriad chilling sounds which rose around me from out of the softly rattling rushes.

A mixture of perfumes assaulted my nostrils, so intense that they seemed almost tangible. *White arrowhead. Iris. Spider lilies. Rafts of yellow pond lilies . . .* My mother had named the swamp flowers to me, wanting to share their remembered beauty.

But there was no beauty for me now. Only the dank, moldering smell of death coupled with the acrid stench of some pungently burning oil.

Suddenly I was alerted. Raising my head, I sniffed the air around me. I had smelled that thick, acrid oiliness before, the night I had watched Valerie chant over her black bottle.

Sensing that my cousin was somewhere nearby, I rose out of the stiff bed of rushes, pressing forward between the thick clumps of wild cane.

It was a flickering pinpoint of fire which gave her away as it had done before. Creeping cautiously nearer to that faintly waving flame, I crouched in the midst of knife-edged palmetto fronds to watch, seeing Valerie clearly now as she stepped out of shadow into a white wash of moonlight.

Another figure stepped forward, and I heard a sharp, cracking sound: Magda, snapping her whip at the burning bottle lamp which stood before them in a small clearing.

Still crouching, I crept nearer, watching as Valerie stooped to trace a design in the soft swamp mud with her finger.

Softly she began to chant, "Astral fluid of the earth, serve as my magical agent. By the powers of Grand Maître, grant my firmly spoken will." In a clear voice, louder, and with determination, she called upon her Voodoo gods whose names I did not recognize.

Turning then, she faced the black line of the swamp, raising her arm in a swift, beckoning motion. I continued to watch as though I were mesmerized, not knowing what to expect, feeling the hairs on my neck begin to prickle, when a pale form emerged from behind a thick clump of swamp grass, carrying a lighted candle.

Amber. Moving with a queer, floating grace, she bent to plant the candle with her left hand in the center of the cleared circle beside Valerie's burning bottle. I saw then that her right hand was missing.

Amber or Rhea I thought wildly. Whose spirit was it that Valerie had somehow conjured up from the grave? And what of my mother? Where was she? *Where was she?*

Waves of dread washed over me as a dark

memory tried to claim me. Blotting from my mind what I had seen inside the tomb on the night the ghost woman had lured me there, I concentrated my attention on Valerie's wildly imploring incantation.

"By the powers of Ye-We, Wedo, Dangbe, lead us to the treasure." My cousin's voice echoed around me, sounding shrill and unnatural. "Valmir will be mine again when I am rich and Tracey is no longer with us. Magda will have Gabe back again, when Tracey goes; Gabe who shares our Cajun heritage, with a lust for riches as strong as our own."

Magda's whip struck out again at the burning bottle, as Valerie's voice rose ever higher, echoing through my head: "Give us the treasure, Grande Maître. Give us back Valmir. Return Gabe to our fold."

Mad, I thought. *Mad. All of them mad.*

It seemed then that I felt some dark power reach to wrap itself around me and suddenly I was running, veering wildly between the rattling palmettos and rustling cane stalks.

Slime sucked at my slippers, its stench rising around me. Turning, I flung my foot forward, searching for solid ground. But the rise I had followed was no longer there.

Small islands of rustling reeds grew

around me. How long had I leapt from one solid clump to the next without realizing that I no longer had firm footing, in my desperation to flee from the dark Voodoo gods who had seemed suddenly to pursue me?

I went forward, my legs sliding into thick mud which reached to my knees. Numbly I remembered the treacherous quagmires my mother had told me about, fear washing over me in waves when I realized that it was becoming increasingly difficult for me to pull my legs free.

Pausing in yet another futile attempt to gain my bearings, I glimpsed a low, wooden platform rising out of a dark cluster of reeds a short distance from me. An old duck blind, I thought on a wild wave of relief. If the ramshackle wooden structure could support a duck hunter, it could support me.

I took a laborious step forward and another, the thick ooze sucking hungrily at my trembling legs, threatening to pull me under. When it seemed that I could not bring myself to take another struggling step forward, as the ooze seemed suddenly to coil itself around my legs and thighs like some monstrous snake hidden from me beneath the blackly shimmering slime, I gave a last desperate lunge forward.

My groping fingers found the edge of a rotting board, and I clung to the splintery wood exhausted, my aching lungs screaming for air.

I have no idea how long I hung there, buried to my waist in slime, before I became aware of a queer, oily pungence. My first thought was that somehow Valerie had followed me with her dreadful black lamp.

Then, as my weary senses began to clear and I raised my head to look around me, I made out a glistening black pool inside the ancient framework which supported me. There were strange bubbling noises, as small bursts of what I guessed to be swamp gas exploded from beneath the mud's slickly shimmering surface. Vaguely then I remembered that my father had expressed regret that oil had not sprung up on Blackhurst land as it had done on the neighboring plantations. The early settlers had observed oil and gas seepage in the swamps from the beginning, he had said.

The Devil's Well. The name of the legendary quagmire burst to the surface of my mind like the popping little bubbles of gas which rose before me to break through the slickly shining slime.

I attempted to raise myself onto the

wooden framework which surrounded the glimmering pond to see more clearly what I had found, even as instinct told me that here was the real treasure my cousins sought.

Suddenly and without warning, there was a sharp, cracking sound beneath me as I attempted to pry myself free from the ooze. With a growing sense of horror, I realized that the plank which supported me had given way, plunging me deeper into the hungrily sucking slime.

Don't struggle, a voice said to me from out of the past. *If you don't struggle, quicksand won't drag you down. You have to remain perfectly stationary. Father told us never to forget that.* The voice belonged to my mother.

I ceased struggling, feeling the tugging sensation on my body lessen. But I could not stay here like this forever.

I tried to think what I must do. It seemed then that there was no recourse left to me but to scream as loudly as I could on the slim chance that Valerie and Magda would hear and come to my rescue.

But it was neither Valerie nor Magda who appeared in response to my wild cries. It was Valmir.

"Tracey!" Relief went over me in waves

at the sound of his voice. "But it can't be! How in God's name . . ."

Turning my head cautiously I saw him making his way toward me across the scattered clumps of reeds.

"Please hurry," I called to him. "But be careful. It's the quagmire. The Devil's Well."

He paused and I saw him testing the air with his nose.

"Crude," he said then in a queer high voice. "Crude oil!"

He came more quickly then, leaping between the scattered clumps of wild cane, weaving around to approach from its far side the rotted framework which guarded the seeping oil well.

Slowly he worked his way toward me around the rim of the rotting planks. I reached out to him as he drew near to me, clutching desperately at his arm. Grasping my wrist in fingers that wrapped about my bones with a strength like steel, he gave me a violent tug. Then just as quickly, he released me and, disbelievingly, I felt his hands pressing onto my back, thrusting me forward into the wickedly bubbling pool.

I struggled to bring my head above the hideous ooze, feeling a violent tugging sensation wrap itself around me. Tasting the thick, oily slime on my tongue, I screamed for Valmir to save me.

"No, *couzan!*" He laughed his charming laugh, his voice mocking me. "Why should I, when my dream of becoming a wealthy planter is at last within my grasp. Thanks to you, *couzan.*" Again his charming laughter rang around me. "Do you realize how long Valerie and I have been searching? This means everything to us. Everything!"

Carefully, so carefully that my movements were scarcely visible, I reached toward yet another of the ancient planks. My fingers found the splintered wood beneath the surface of the slime and I clung there helplessly, Valmir's insanely charming laughter ringing softly around me.

"It was you all along," I said numbly. "In San Francisco . . ."

"Yes, *couzan.* I've worked hard for this. It seemed imperative that I intercept Lorainne's letters after I'd gone to so much trouble to see that the telephone lines were out of order. It wasn't easy, with Gabe interfering."

"You're the one who met my mother's bus the night of her arrival," I said, the pieces beginning at last to fall into place.

"I had equipped myself with one of

Valerie's obeah death potions in preparation for what was to follow," Valmir said. "I mixed it into the thermos of coffee I was thoughtful enough to prepare for Lorainne to help revive her after her long journey. She had to die, you know."

But I had received the letters from her after that, I thought on a queer surge of dread. How? How could she write to me if she were already dead?

"The potion didn't work," Valmir said as though he had seen into my tumultuous thoughts. "I was forced to lock Lorainne away in the west wing where she kept company with Amber's ghost."

"There are no such things as ghosts," I whispered uncertainly.

"Amber betrayed me by making friends with Lorainne," Valmir said, without hearing me. "It was Amber who smuggled out the letters Lorainne wrote to you. I found out too late that she had left them in the box out by the gate for the postman to pick up on his daily rounds."

"My mother . . . Where is she now?" I asked, a small wave of hope rising up in me.

"With Amber," Valmir said. "I used the necklace with its curse to hasten her departure to that other world. It was easy after that to catch a plane to San Francisco on the pretense of going to Baton Rouge to do some research on the Blackhurst history. Everyone here knows how fond I am of the old stories."

Valmir, then, had been Mrs. Costain's foreign-looking stranger, I thought. Not Gabe. *Not Gabe!*

Suddenly I wanted desperately to live.

"Please, Valmir! Help me!" I cried.

"Don't be frightened, Tracey," he said softly. "You will be with them. With Lorainne and Amber."

"But why? Why must you leave me here to die?" I gasped, the ooze pressing insistently around me.

"Because you are the owner of Blackhurst Hall," he said. "Grandfather left it to Lorainne, stipulating that Seena be allowed to remain in the house until she dies. Now Lorainne is dead. That leaves you, *couzan*. Grandfather made it clear in his will that everything was to go to you in the event of Lorainne's death. You are all that stands between me and the kind of life I want, the life I must have. So you see, *couzan*, I have no real choice in the matter."

I knew then that it was hopeless to plead with him. It seemed then as I watched him turn away, that my only chance for survival lay in the off-chance that someone would venture into the swamps to look for me and that eventually I would be found.

Little by little, as the hours dragged endlessly by, hope slipped away. I lay in slime to my armpits, clinging feebly to the rotted planks with hands that had long since gone numb.

Then suddenly there was a whisper of sound, a soft voice calling, "Lorainne! I've found you at last! I've found you."

Cautiously raising my head, I peered between the coarse clumps of swamp grass beyond the board framework.

The ghost woman came toward me, her bridal gown and veil floating eerily above the blank fingers of slime that threaded between the small grass islands.

Amber. I must have spoken her name aloud, for she paused then to look at me.

"You know," she said. "You know I lost my hand. Like Rhea," she added.

Like Rhea. Miss Rhea has reddish-colored hair, poor thing, Odalie had said.

Has! Rhea wasn't dead then, I thought wildly. It was Rhea who lived in the west wing, not Amber's ghost, as those who lived in the old house had wanted me to believe.

I called to her. "Please, Rhea. Go get help. I'm your cousin Tracey, Lorainne's daughter."

"The letters were for you," she said. "But the will is mine. Do you understand? Mine! I took it from the place where Valmir had put it for safekeeping and hid it where he will never think to look. Lorainne knows where it is. She's the only one. She knows the plantation has to belong to me, after all these years. The plantation belongs to Amber now."

"But you're Rhea," I said.

"I was Lorainne's only friend," she said in a strange soft voice, like a sleeper awaking from a dream. "I promised her I would help you when you came, if she was gone by then."

"Please, help me then," I said gently.

Before I could stop her, Rhea plunged suddenly toward me, sinking into the mire. Grasping a rotted board with her left hand, she struggled clumsily to free it, bracing on a nearby timber with the stump of her right arm.

I heard a splintering crash as the plank she had tried to pry away broke free. Reaching for the loosened piece, she thrust it at me, wading nearer, the amber beads swinging wildly around her neck.

Then suddenly she was sinking, the white veil she wore spreading across the black ooze like some huge exotic lily.

I screamed then. And screamed again. And suddenly there was Valmir, leaping swiftly between the solid clumps of grass. I saw Rhea's left hand reach out of the slime to grasp his ankle and he went flying.

Helplessly I watched as the two of them struggled together in the midst of the loudly sucking ooze.

Then suddenly they were gone and there were only the soft bubbling sounds of the Devil's Well bursting around me.

It was Gabe who found me. I still shudder to think what might have happened had he not come when he did to pull me out of the ooze to safety. The rest of that night passed in a blur. Vaguely I recall sensing the activity around me as I lay in my mother's bed, my senses soothed by the tranquilizing drug Dr. Whitaker had arrived to give me.

Valmir and Rhea's bodies were never found. It was as though the earth had opened to swallow them, which in a sense it had. Plans were made for a memorial service and when that was over, Seena came to me to admit that her continuing jealousy of my mother had been only a subterfuge to keep Lorainne away from Blackhurst Hall so she would never have to know the truth about Rhea.

During the brief time my mother had been at the house to attend my grandmother's funeral, she had happened to catch a glimpse of my older cousin dressed in Amber's wedding gown, Seena went on to explain. I knew then why there had seemed to be a change in my mother's attitude when she had returned to my father and me in San Francisco. She must have wondered, as I had done, whether or not there actually was a ghost, in the wake of the terrible legend that had grown up around that first bride.

As for my cousins, Valerie and Magda, they had known about Rhea, of course. Her ghostly presence in the west wing had had its effect on them all. But it was Valmir who had been most deeply affected. Seena and Valerie both had guessed what was happening as Valmir came gradually to believe Rhea was actually Amber. Perhaps that was the only way he could live with himself, considering the way he had used her, I thought.

But it was not until Gabe came to me and told me that the reason he had offered to buy any share I might have in the plantation was because he had begun to feel my life was endangered that I at last felt the evil power which had seemed to surround me begin to lift.

As witness to my grandfather's will, Gabe had known that the plantation would belong to me in the event of my mother's death. It had been his intention to return any share I might have blindly agreed to sell him, in the event the will turned up, as he was certain it must eventually do.

"I took it upon myself to look after you," he said. "But I didn't do a very good job of it, did I, to let all of those frightening things happen to you?"

"I wish you'd had a chance to watch over my mother," I said wistfully. "None of this would have happened, had she managed to contact you as it was her intention to do."

"Unfortunately, Valmir got to her first," Gabe said. "I'd heard Seena speak of her sister, of course. But I'd never met your mother. Nor had I any idea that she had actually come here to Blackhurst Hall that first night when I met you wandering like a lost waif along the pecan alley. I only began to suspect later that something like that might have been the case. Valmir succeeded only too well in keeping any knowledge of her presence here from us. And to think that he very nearly succeeded in duplicating his evil deeds where you were concerned." Gabe reached to draw me to him.

"You couldn't watch me every minute," I said.

"I intend to after this," he told me.

I said, "Even if it should be proved that I'm not an heiress after all?"

"But there is no way we can prove that, is there, so I'll have to take my chances," he said, bending to kiss me.

"In that case, I'll tell you where the will is hidden," I said.

He gave me a stunned look. Taking his hand, I led him toward Blackhurst's library.

The book containing the lines from Fuller was there, as I had known it would be, behind leaded-glass doors. I opened it to the page which contained the quotation from the *Life of Monica.*

The will was taped to the top of the page, a last legacy of love from my mother.

The shadow of death has lifted from the old mansion at last. In a little while, Gabe will come and we will be married in the garden beneath a bower of myrtle, symbol of eternal love.

About the Author

Monica Heath lives with her husband on what was once one of the original Gold Rush claims in the western United States. Her novel, *Woman in Black*, grew out of her intense interest in the history of that era. Of Irish descent, she calls on her racial heritage to create many of the characters who appear in her stories. An artist as well as a writer, she is the mother of three children.

We hope you have enjoyed this Large Print book. Other Thorndike, Wheeler or Chivers Press Large Print books are available at your library or directly from the publishers.

For more information about current and upcoming titles, please call or write, without obligation, to:

Publisher
Thorndike Press
295 Kennedy Memorial Drive
Waterville, ME   04901
Tel. (800) 223-1244

Or visit our Web site at:
www.gale.com/thorndike
www.gale.com/wheeler

OR

Chivers Large Print
published by BBC Audiobooks Ltd
St James House, The Square
Lower Bristol Road
Bath BA2 3SB
England
Tel. +44(0) 800 136919
email: bbcaudiobooks@bbc.co.uk
www.bbcaudiobooks.co.uk

All our Large Print titles are designed for easy reading, and all our books are made to last.